WHO

KILLED

MAGGIE

SWIFT?

ꟼP

WHO KILLED MAGGIE SWIFT?

The Frank May Chronicles

Lawrence Friedman

A QP Mystery

QP BOOKS
New Orleans, Louisiana

WHO KILLED MAGGIE SWIFT?
The Frank May Chronicles

A QP Mystery, published in 2014 by QP Books.

QUID PRO, LLC
5860 Citrus Blvd., Suite D-101
New Orleans, Louisiana 70123
www.qpbooks.com

ISBN 978·1·61027·224·7 (pbk.)
ISBN 978·1·61027·225·4 (eBook)

Publisher's Cataloging-in-Publication

Friedman, Lawrence.

Who Killed Maggie Swift? / Lawrence Friedman.

p. cm.

Series: *The Frank May Chronicles* (#7)

ISBN: 978-1-61027-224-7 (pbk.)

1. Lawyers—California—Fiction. 2. San Mateo (Cal.)—Fiction. 3. May, Frank (Fictitious character)—Fiction. I. Friedman, Lawrence. II. Title. III. Series.

PS357.F781 2014

833.'1'8292—dc22

20140453887

CIP

*for Leah, Jane, Amy, Sarah,
David, Lucy, and Irene*

WHO
KILLED
MAGGIE
SWIFT?

1

It's a known fact that people don't like to go to the dentist. Mind you, it's not as bad as it used to be. Modern dentists have great equipment, they've got these high speed drills, they use painkillers (OK, we don't like the needle), they try to make things as non-traumatic as they possibly can. Still, going to the dentist—it's just not something you look forward to. In my experience, people don't hesitate to cancel an appointment. Not that I'm a dentist—I'm a lawyer—but I'm basing my judgment on personal experience: me, my family, and my circle of friends. My wife, Celia, never cancels, but she's a person with a strong character. Most people are adept at making up excuses for canceling, unless they have a real toothache or other emergency. Otherwise, they try to weasel out. It's almost as bad as the lengths they go to avoid jury service. People with dental appointments claim headaches, fevers, out-of-town trips—even jury duty. Any excuse for putting off the visit.

Anyway, this story begins with me, Frank May, and a late morning appointment with my dentist, Dr. Caleb Colegrove. His office is directly across the street from mine, in downtown San Mateo, California. It was an appointment I didn't keep. But I defy anybody to think of a reason more dramatic than the one I had for missing my appointment with Dr. Colegrove. I was in my office, working away. It was morning, and I had an appointment, as I said, for late morning: I was scheduled for just before lunch. In the morning, I heard sirens wailing, but paid no attention; I'm on a busy street, and we hear sirens all the time. But then when I stepped out onto the street, later on, in order to drag myself over to the dentist's place, I saw police cars, and a small crowd of people standing in front of the building where Dr. Colegrove had his office. In short, I never got to see the dentist that day. I never had my teeth X-rayed, never had the plaque removed, never heard my annual lecture about flossing.

All the appointments that day were canceled. And for a very good reason. Sometime in the morning Maggie, the receptionist, a sweet lady with white hair and a nice plump face, was found dead in the office. Maggie, in fact, had died a violent death. The police called it murder.

As I said, I happen to be a lawyer. One of my fellow lawyers, E. Stanley Banks, whose office is just down the block, was the one who actually found the body. Stanley and I were once on a committee together—bar association business. Stanley's practice overlaps with mine, a bit; we both do wills, trusts, and estates. But mainly he does shopping centers. He's an old-time lawyer, very respectable, a man in his 70's I'd say, but still putting in a full day at the office.

"It was horrible," he told me, when we had coffee together a day or so later.

"You were there for an appointment?"

He hesitated for a minute, which I found a bit odd. But then he said, "Yes, I came for my appointment, regular appointment, I go every six months, you know, they clean your teeth, sometimes they take X-rays. I'm very fussy about my teeth. My cousin Max had to have three teeth pulled—he never went to the dentist, years at a time, it was just plain neglect. I go religiously. I had an implant last year, with Dr. Frost. Charged an arm and a leg but it's like a real tooth. Dr. Colegrove referred me. But never mind. Anyway, I came to the building, you know, to Dr. Colegrove's office, and the door was locked. Funny thing. Right away, I saw something was wrong."

"Something wrong?"

"I mean, why was the door locked? Regular business hours; it shouldn't be locked. So I walked around the block, and thought, I'll try again, and then it was open, and usually there's two women there, the receptionist, Maggie, and another woman, I forget her name, Maggie is at the desk, and she's also calling people, you know, reminding them of appointments. The other woman, she's mostly doing something with the records or the files or whatever. I think they spell each other off, sometimes, but every time I went there, I saw the two of them. There's another lady too, I see her once in a while, but these two were the main ones, I think. Then there's Charlotte, the dental assistant. I didn't see her. Well, as I said, nobody was there. I thought, that's funny; but maybe they stepped out. So I sat down in the waiting room, and I picked up a magazine. I think it was *National Geographic*. I waited a bit, and then I had to go to the bathroom. There's two of them, one near the front and one in back. Naturally, I went to the front one, and I went in there ... and, I mean, this was totally horrible, that's where I saw it. The body. Maggie's body."

"My God, Stanley, how awful."

"Don't I know it? It's something you don't forget. Gave me nightmares, I swear. Look—I was unzipping my fly, you know, getting ready to urinate, I have an enlarged prostate, I could take pills, but I don't want to. Anyway, a guy my age, you never pass up a urinal. So there I was, and I thought I saw something in the stall, and I bent down to look, I mean after I got done with my business, and oh God, it was a woman's foot—the back of a foot, without a shoe. And I thought, what's going on here, so I opened the door of the stall, and she was lying there, face down, you know, I mean, her face was sort of by the toilet bowl—blood all over. I started yelling and yelling, Dr. Colegrove came, and then we called the police; and I forgot all the time, my fly was open, God knows what people were thinking."

"Wow, Stanley, that's incredible. Truly awful." Meanwhile, I thought, that could have been me. I could have been the one who found the dead body. I could have been the one whose fly was open. Thank God Stanley had an earlier appointment.

"I knew Maggie," I said.

"You knew her?"

"No. I mean, yes. I knew her from Dr. Colegrove's office. She seemed awfully nice. Friendly. Why would anybody want to kill her?"

Stanley said he had no idea. He said, "I knew her too. Slightly. She once spoke to me, professionally."

I wondered about that, but let it pass. I wouldn't have thought Maggie needed a lawyer; but you never can tell. I was too absorbed in thinking about the whole terrible business. Why would somebody do an awful thing like that? That was precisely the question I asked, later at home, to my wife Celia. We've been married twenty years.

She said: "Robbery, maybe? I mean, drugs? Don't dentists keep drugs, you know, things they use for anesthesia?"

Actually, I had no idea.

"And did you tell me, she didn't have any shoes on?"

"I did."

"Why would somebody take off her shoes? And where were the shoes?" I had no answer, of course.

"I have to talk to Chloe," she said. "What a shock that must be."

Chloe was Celia's cousin. Or rather the daughter of Celia's cousin, which makes her a cousin once-removed. Chloe's mother lived in Bakersfield, which is in the Central Valley. Chloe couldn't wait to leave the nest. If you knew Bakersfield, you wouldn't wonder. She worked in Dr. Colegrove's office, as a receptionist. Part-time. The rest of the time, she was a student at De Anza, a community college. She was studying something called marketing. I know that products have to be marketed, but frankly, I can't imagine what a course in marketing might consist of. I never asked Chloe. Doesn't matter. Anyway, since Chloe worked for Caleb Colegrove, that made her a very special person at this point in time.

Of course, on my block in downtown San Mateo, the murder was the sole topic of conversation, as you might imagine. Felicity, the waitress in the coffee shop next door, was positively obsessed with it. "You know, she came here all the time. Maggie. She liked a low-fat latte. Once in a while she had a blueberry scone. She just loved blueberry scones."

"Did you talk to her?" I asked, over my mid-morning coffee.

"Sometimes. It's usually too busy here. She told me blueberries were healthy, that's why she ate those scones. Full of antioxidants, whatever those are. She told me to eat blueberries. But they're so expensive, especially in winter. Anyway, Maggie, poor thing. She was so worried about her health. About her weight, too.... And now she's dead."

Felicity had a hard life. She had told me all about it. Her husband left her; she had a handicapped child of some sort, and a mother with Alzheimer's. Naturally, she had money problems. I don't imagine the job paid very well. She wore her dyed hair piled up on top of her head. I would say she was between 40 and 50.

Ironic; for people like Felicity, Maggie's murder was a godsend. Something to get excited about, something to talk to the customers about. A jolt of energy in a dismal life. Imagine, her coffee shop—Joanna's Café—right across the street from where a murder took place. She could tell this to her neighbors and the customers. She could tell them, too, that she knew Maggie, the woman who got murdered. She could tell them how Maggie used to come in and sit right down and talk to her. How she sat at the counter, not in a booth. Felicity could spread the word about the blueberry scones. She was—what's the word—on the inside. Maybe for the first time in her life.

Me, this crime just made me sad. The poor woman. Who on earth could have killed her?

It never occurred to me, then, that I would get involved. Deeply involved. So much so that, at the end, there were those who thought I was the one who cracked the case open. That's debatable. I'll let you be the judge of that.

Let me introduce myself. My name is Frank May. As I told you, I'm an attorney, a member of the California bar. I have a small office in downtown San Mateo: that's a suburb, a few miles to the south of San Francisco. I have a wife—I think I mentioned that already—and two teenaged daughters. Thank God they have nothing to do with the case.

My wife is a high school teacher. People like her deserve the Medal of Honor. I think I would rather step into a lion cage than face a roomful of sullen adolescents, which she does day in and day out.

I have a general practice of law—I'm a jack of all trades. Well, not quite. I don't do criminal law; that's highly specialized. Or patents. Too technical. Indeed, what I mostly do is handle estates: wills, trusts, conservatorships, guardianships. Somehow my practice evolved in that direction. It's a nice little branch of practice. It keeps me solvent. I have no complaints.

When I came home that evening, Chloe was there in the living room, talking to Celia. Chloe was short and somewhat dumpy. She always wore long, complicated earrings. I never saw her without them. I don't like complicated earrings. Chloe was, in my opinion, neither very bright nor very attractive. But blood, as Celia used to say, is thicker than water. She felt sorry for Chloe. "Her father was a gambler. Left them all penniless, Chloe, her mom, and her two sisters. It was a struggle to survive." The mother was Celia's cousin. The gambler was not a relative at all, I'm pleased to say.

Chloe was eating a sandwich, which Celia had made for her. But she could hardly contain her excitement. "I mean, a real murder. And poor Maggie. Whoever could have done that to her? I'm sure it was this mystery man."

"Mystery man?"

"Oh, Celia, it's so exciting. Scary too, but... it's just like a movie. Really. Like something out of a movie. This is what happened. At the time, we didn't think too much about it, but now.... It was this new patient, Celia. I'm sure he was the one."

"What new patient?"

"Well, this man called up, and he wanted an appointment. He said he'd never been to the doctor before. He said his name was Hendrik Borromeo. Funny name, don't you think? We had to ask him to spell it. Nobody saw him, it was just over the phone, he talked to me, I was answering the phone—I mean, Maggie was there, but I was the one. Anyway, he had a funny voice, at the time I hardly noticed it, but now I think he was disguising his voice. He said a friend recommended Dr. Colegrove. Well, there's nothing funny about that, it happens all the time. He said he was new in town. He needed a dental checkup. We asked him, did he have a dental plan, and he said, no he didn't, not yet anyway. He didn't have a permanent address yet, he said. I asked for a phone number, and he gave me a number, he said it was his cell phone.

"Then he asked me something really odd, he asked me if Maggie was there, and I said, oh, yes, do you know her? And he said, well, she's a friend of a friend, and I said do you want to talk to her, and he said no, no, it isn't necessary. And he was supposed to come in that awful day, you know, the day Maggie died; but he never showed up. I mean, I think he didn't. And the police wanted to know, the list of the patients, I mean, the ones that were coming in that day, so I gave them the list, and I mentioned this guy, Hendrik Borromeo, and gave them the phone number. They told me later there was no such number, was I sure I had the right number? Don't you think that's awfully suspicious? No address, and a fake telephone number. Of course, I could have gotten the number wrong. But I don't think so."

Celia asked her if she wanted another sandwich—roast beef or turkey, either one. She chose roast beef.

I said, "Chloe, so you think this man, this Hendrik person, you think he's the one that killed Maggie?"

"Well, I think the police think so too. They came back, and they asked me all sorts of questions. But of course I didn't know anything. It was just a voice on the phone...."

"Was this person old or young?"

"I really don't know. I don't think he was old. I mean, not an old man's voice, all crinkly, you know how that is. Well, I mean, not a very old man. It could have been somebody... oh, I just don't know. Of course, now I think maybe it was somebody stalking the place.... Maybe there never was any such person. Not under that name, anyway. It's creepy."

"Did you... see the body? Were you there that morning?"

Chloe shuddered. "Oh, thank God, no, I saw nothing.... I mean, I had morning classes, I don't usually have classes in the morning, I try to take mostly courses at night, but this one course, it met in the morning. Ten o'clock class. So that semester I told Dr. Colegrove, I'd come in later, Tuesdays and Thursdays. When I came in, the police were there, I think they took the body away already. A big crowd of people outside the front door. Well, you saw that, Frank. I remember, you came out... Anyway, I was scared. And the questions they asked me! Like, where was I? That morning. As if they thought, maybe I was the one who killed her, can you imagine? I told them, I was in class. They said, can anybody 'corroborate' that? That's the word they used, 'corroborate.'"

"You poor thing."

"Well, of course, I'm not worried. Ms. Fishpond can

tell them I was there, the whole time, in the class. Anyway, the thing was so utterly horrible. Her head was all smashed in, that's what I heard. I said to this man—I don't know who he was, at first, anyway, just that he was with the police—I said, well, maybe it was an accident, she fell down, cracked her head open. And he just shook his head, like, no ma'am, not an accident. And he said he was from the homicide squad, so they think, for sure, it was a murder."

In many ways, it must have been traumatic for Chloe. And yet... on the other hand, she was like Felicity, and even closer to the epicenter: it was a source of enormous excitement. Poor Maggie's death was a thrilling event. I tried to imagine what Chloe's life was like. Did she have friends? More to the point, did she have boyfriends? Celia used to say, she wished Chloe would lose weight. "She won't get anybody, because she's fat."

I said, "She's not that fat. Don't exaggerate."

"Fat enough," Celia said.

2

The next morning, when I went to work, I couldn't resist walking across the street to look at the building where it all happened. It was a two story building, stucco mostly; there was nothing special about it. It was a plain, ordinary, commercial building—there are thousands of them in the world. Clean, with a small lawn and decent flowers. I would imagine it was well-managed.

Dr. Colegrove's dental office was on the first floor. I tried to remember the layout. First, there was a small room, where the receptionists sat; along with a tiny sitting area, equipped with out-of-date magazines, and a few toys for kids who might have been dragged in. Many is the time I sat in that small space, waiting, looking at his rather shabby collection of magazines. Dr. Colegrove subscribed to something called Golf Digest, and for those who were interested, a magazine called Modern Dentistry. Caleb had once had a knee replacement, and he seemed to have kept on, from those days, a subscription to a journal called the Lower Extremity Review. The lead article was on "The Significance of Squatting." I sighed and picked up an old National Geographic, featuring a story about "Blind Cave Salamanders of Appalachia." This was as good as I could do, as far as magazines were concerned.

The fatal bathroom was just off to the right of the place where the receptionists sat. There was a corridor, to the left of the office, and this led to a wing that housed the actual dental torture chambers. Four rooms or so—I couldn't remember exactly how many—with the usual dental equipment. Dr. Colegrove used one of the bigger rooms. There was a younger dentist too, and two dental assistants, the ones that cleaned your teeth. Maybe it was five rooms. And there was another bathroom in the back, somewhere; I don't think I ever used it.

Dr. Colegrove had been my dentist for years. He had been in partnership with an older man, Dr. Morris Sylvester. Dr. Sylvester died a few years back. Dr. Colegrove took on a new partner, a young man named Ryan Dobbs. I hardly knew him. I dealt exclusively with Dr. Colegrove.

There were two receptionists, as I recall—Maggie, and another woman, who split the job with Maggie; and then there was Chloe, who helped out, part-time. There were at least two dental assistants. One of them was named Charlotte; she's the only one I was familiar with. There was another one, named Estelle.

I looked at the building's directory. There were other dentists on the second floor, including a periodontist named Hiram Whistler. And an office occupied by Wishbone and Wishbone: Investment Counselors. The main floor was divided into two sections, which were not closely connected, although I suppose it would be easy to go from one section to the other. The other section contained the offices of a company called the Xyloquex Corporation. I had no idea what Xyloquex did for a living. If you're a periodontist, or an Investment Counselor, you proclaim this fact on the building directory, and on the door to your office; but Xyloquex revealed nothing other than its name to the outside world.

I imagined Xyloquex had something to do with computers, but this was a sheer guess. Xyloquex could be anything. Well, almost anything. You can't imagine a real estate company or a financial institution of any kind calling itself Xyloquex. High-tech companies, on the other hand, seemed to like names like Xyloquex. They like x's, q's and z's. At least that's the way it seems to me.

As I was standing in front of the building, a young man came out the door. He was wearing blue jeans and a turtle-neck sweater. He was thin, with a pointy nose and dirty blond hair. He took out a package of cigarettes and lit one. He looked to be about 18 or 19. I recalled having seen him before, smoking his cigarette outside the building. You notice such things in California. People don't smoke in California. They may do yoga or run in marathons or eat vegan food or all of these things; but cigarettes are a total taboo. A person might very well smoke pot, I suppose, but tobacco? Never.

I said, "Hello." He grunted an answer. I asked him, "Do you work in the building?"

He said something that sounded like yes and puffed on his cigarette. I asked again, and he said, "Yeah. I do."

"Can I ask you, who do you work for?"

He gave me a sullen look. Young people are frequently sullen. Teenagers in particular. Or maybe it's only when they talk to people over 30. "Hey, man, what's it to you, where I work?"

"Nothing special," I said. "It's just, well, you know what happened in the building.... That woman, the one who was killed."

He looked at me suspiciously. He said: "That was the lady who worked for the dentist. I don't work for that guy. I had nothing to do with it."

I said, "I didn't think you did.... I mean, it's just that... well, you were in the building, weren't you?"

He said: "I work for Xyloquex."

I wanted to ask what he did for them, and what kind of company it was, and why they called themselves by that ridiculous name; but I felt I couldn't bring this up at the moment. He apparently decided to be at least minimally friendly: "I'm Judd," he said.

I said, "I'm Frank. I work across the way. I'm a lawyer."

"Yeah? A lawyer? Wow."

I said: "Terrible thing, in your building, wasn't it?"

He looked at me suspiciously. Like, why is this man asking questions? But then he said: "Yeah. Right. Hey, you know, I saw the lady, honest to God, it must have been just before she died. I mean, I went out on the street, right over there down the street, there's a bench there by the bus stop, and I was smoking a cigarette. I know, you're not supposed to smoke. The boss hates it. He's not around much, he's some kind of German guy. I'm trying to stop. I told my mom, I'm going to stop. Anyway, she came out of the building, I mean, not my mom, but this lady, and she said, hello Judd. I mean, not that I knew her that all well, but I saw her a few times, and I asked her once, something about the dentist, I don't like dentists, like, you know, who does? But I had this toothache, it was just about killing me, and she talked about Dr. Colegrove: she said, well, don't you have a dentist? And I said, yeah, but not here, I just moved here from Phoenix, and I'm looking for a dentist. And she said, oh, you should go to Dr. Colegrove, he's a wonderful dentist. Anyway, that was that one time. Anyway, the toothache went away, and I don't have dental insurance, I don't get benefits from this lousy place I work for, so I never went. This time, I was just sitting on the bench, and I saw her come out...."

"Where was she going? What was she doing?"

"Man, how would I know? I didn't think anything about it, at the time. I mean, I had lots of stuff on my mind. She could have been going anywhere, you know? Was none of my business, I'm not nosy."

He tossed the cigarette onto the pavement and ground it with his shoe. "I better get back to work," he said, and went into the building.

I thought about what Judd had told me. If he was telling the truth, Judd was an important witness. He saw Maggie leave the building. Nobody knows why she did that; it seemed strange, because it meant she was leaving the office completely empty, at least the reception desk. Then she must have gone back in, because somebody killed her, after all. It couldn't have happened outside, that was a ridiculous idea—I mean, the idea that somebody killed her, on the streets of San Mateo in broad daylight, and brought her back to the office to put her in a toilet stall.

Meanwhile, while this was going on, the murder and all that, Dr. Colegrove was somewhere in the office complex, drilling somebody's teeth, or whatever. Did he kill Maggie? But why would he? Or somebody crept into the office, the door was open, nobody was there at the moment, and maybe hid in the bathroom. Then when Maggie came back and went into the bathroom, that person killed her. But again, why on earth? And at some point, the door was closed; that's what Stanley said.

All this was food for thought. At any rate, I hadn't gotten any closer to finding out what Xyloquex did for a living. Whatever it was, Judd was unlikely to be high up on the chain of command. I know, there are people Judd's age who drop out of high school and make a billion dollars with some marvelous computer breakthrough or a start-up that gets sold to Google or Apple and makes them enormously rich. Judd, alas, did not fit the profile of a computer geek or a genius at software. He was more the type who flipped burgers at McDonald's. A genuine drop-out from life.

3

When I got back to the office, I had a message on my phone from Dr. Colegrove himself. I should mention that he was a client of mine, not just my dentist. Caleb Colegrove had once been married to a woman named Lucille. Not a happy marriage. Lucille produced a daughter for Caleb, but Caleb and Lucille grew increasingly distant from each other. At least that was Caleb's story. One never knows. At any rate, when the daughter was about twelve or thirteen, Lucille ran off with a computer repairman, who apparently made house calls. At least he made house calls for Lucille. Anyway, she ran off with him, and they moved to Bozeman, Montana, because the guy loved to hunt and fish. Were there enough computers to fix in Bozeman? I suppose this is possible. Computers are everywhere. The daughter went with them. She never liked Caleb. He said: "Lucille, she poisoned the child's mind."

I heard the whole story, in excruciating detail.

Anyway, Caleb came to me, after all of this, because he needed to revise his will. His original will left everything to his wife, except for a small sum for his Aunt Bernice. Now Bernice was dead and the wife was off in Bozeman. Caleb said he wanted to provide for his daughter. "She doesn't care for me, I know that; and I never see her. Never. But she's my flesh and blood, Frank." He also wanted to make sure that Lucille never got her hands on any of his money. "I paid her enough.

She took me to the cleaners."

We talked about a trust, and I assured him we could set it up so that Lucille would have no role whatsoever. "Neither would Phil, of course," I said.

"Phil?"

"Isn't that the name of her, uh, partner? The computer guy?"

"God, he's history. He didn't last. He got rid of Lucille. He ran off with some tramp, some waitress or something. Now he's in Idaho. Boise I think. Serves her right, Lucille. But she bounced right back, I'm sorry to say. Found herself a new guy, believe it or not, a master plumber. Makes me think, does she screw anybody who comes to the house to fix things?"

I had no comment to make. Her first love, of course, was Caleb Colegrove, a dentist. A dentist fixes things. Doesn't come to the house, though. And a dentist, in this snobbish world, is a cut above plumbers, I suppose. Or computer repairmen.

Anyway, two can play at that particular game. I mean the game of love. Dr. Colegrove found himself a new wife, Sandra. I never met the woman. They say she was much younger than he was. They also said that she was rich. Whether this was true or not, I have no idea. All I know about her is that Caleb came to see me once again, also to change his will, and leave at least part of his assets to Sandra.

At any rate, on this particular day, I got this message from Caleb. He said he needed to talk to me, and could I possibly come by later on? Or he could come to my office. His last patient would be gone by 5:30, he said. I called back and told the receptionist—Maggie's replacement, I assume—that I would come to his office at 5:30. Frankly, I wanted to see the scene of the crime; I had been there before, of course, but never paid that much attention. It was now an object of enormous interest.

I did feel vaguely guilty. We were having company for

dinner, and I know Celia would want me home as early as possible. She had invited her colleague, Adam Finkel, the math teacher, "you know, the one with the terrible skin problem." He brought out the mother instinct in Celia. She was fond of Adam; consequently, I was on thin ice saying yes to Caleb Colegrove and making a late afternoon appointment. So why did I do it? You know why. Dr. Colegrove was in the eye of a hurricane of fascinating news. How could I, a mere mortal, turn down the chance to inch closer to the heart of this mystery?

In retrospect, I should have hurried home and made small talk with Adam Finkel, trying hard not to notice his terrible skin. I would have spared myself a lot of grief.

I arrived at Dr. Colegrove's office right on time. The receptionists and dental assistants had already gone home. Caleb was sitting in the front office, thumbing through a magazine. He was a rather handsome man with a very professional, distinguished look. A full head of hair, somewhat gray at the temples. He was especially impressive when he wore his white coat, which was the way I usually saw him. I'd guess his age to be about 50, give or take a few years. I could look this up in my files, but it hardly seems relevant.

"Frank," he said. "It's good of you to come. I need your help. This thing is awful. Really awful. I mean, Maggie.... What a tragedy. And the police, the questions, the newspaper reporters. An absolute nightmare. You can't imagine how upset my wife is, Sandra, she's in therapy anyway. And... my reputation...."

"I'm so sorry," I said. "I really am. It must have been a terrible shock."

"Oh yes, absolutely dreadful. Can you imagine? Funny thing, I thought at first, this is bad for business. We had to cancel everybody that day, and this was serious—in the afternoon, there was this woman with an impacted molar, and I had to tell her to go elsewhere... well, never mind. But here's the funny thing: yes, that day it was bad for business. But then: turns out it's good for business. The publicity.... The newspapers called me a leading dentist. You can't buy that kind of publicity. I'm booked solid. I have a whole flock of new patients. But you think I like it? Not really. Believe me, Frank, it's not as if I had no patients before this all happened. I don't want you to think I'm callous. I was very, very fond of Maggie. A lovely woman. All of this.... It's a total nightmare. You can't begin to know how much of a nightmare."

"I can imagine."

"Can you? I don't think so. I dread going to the office, I swear. I have these new patients, you wouldn't believe what they're like. This woman, she must be around 50, she was Dr. Flansbaum's patient, she said she wanted to change, he ruined my fillings, she said. Nonsense. He does very careful work, and when I looked, there was nothing wrong inside her mouth. All she wanted was to talk about the murder. She told me I was very sexy, can you imagine? For a minute I was afraid she was going to take her clothes off, and she was wearing the shortest skirt I've ever seen. A woman of her age. Her name was Linda. A married woman, I actually know her husband. Well, slightly. Anyway, I called in Charlotte, you know, my dental assistant, I think she worked with you—she's the one with the reddish hair. I made up some excuse, I just didn't want to be alone with that woman. The only way I could get her to stop talking was to make her keep her mouth open.... That's our secret weapon, you know...."

I nodded my head in agreement. Where was this going?

He went on: "Well, the worst of it is, the police and all of that. Questions, questions. Of course I suppose I'm a suspect. They're probably looking into my background, did I ever do anything violent, how about that fat boy I punched in high school, God knows what else. Some people around here think I killed her. Can you believe it? Me? I mean, it's the craziest thing I ever heard. Harvey Wishbone—you know, the investment counselor, the one in our building, my wife and I use him, he came in, he told me he was so sorry about Maggie; then he said, yes, what a tragedy, and besides that, there's all these terrible rumors. And I said, what rumors? He said, well, maybe you don't want to know. But I do, I said to him. I've got to know what people are saying. Well, it's my clients, he said, and some of them are big gossips. I said to him, Harvey, tell me, what are they gossiping about? He was pretty hesitant, Harvey, and then he told me: it's all kind of nonsense. Like, for instance, that this woman was my lover, we were having sex in the restroom, and I killed her, it was some kind of sex game, something kinky, you know, something like that thing years ago, they called it the preppy murder, do you remember it?"

In fact I didn't.

Caleb went on: "This kid, I can't think of his name, he choked this girl, killed her, it was some sort of kinky sex. Choking somebody when you have sex. It's supposed to be a big thrill. The things people do. I couldn't believe what Harvey was telling me. I said, they think it was something like that? I said, Harvey, the woman was 70 years old if she was a day, please, give me credit for some taste in women."

I shook my head solemnly, to express solidarity.

He said: "I don't know where they get such ideas. Completely crazy. And there are other rumors, too. Who knows what. Satanic cults, for God's sake. Somebody told me about a new one, a new rumor, that the office, it's being investigated, some huge scandal—dental malpractice, insurance fraud—and Maggie was on to something, she had to be shut up. By me, presumably. At least I have some idea why people might think that way."

"You do, Caleb?"

"There's a lawsuit against me, malpractice, it's completely groundless, but it's there. The claim is, I killed a patient, I'm incompetent, and so on. Yes, I had a patient and he died suddenly, the anesthetic—let's not go into it. But the idea that I covered it up, and Maggie knew about it, or she was blackmailing me or whatever.... Frank, if this goes on, Sandra will have a nervous breakdown. She's so fragile as it is. God... we have issues anyway, me and Sandra. To be honest, Frank, my marriage is unraveling. This is all I need to finish it off."

I told him again how sorry I was.

"And Harvey himself says, he saw a man going into the office, right about the time Maggie must have been killed. I said, what sort of man, old, young, what? And he said, he had no idea, just a glimpse. He thought the man was wearing blue jeans, not that that's anything of a help. Who knows? Maybe Harvey killed her for all I know."

I said, "Harvey? Why would he do that? Anyway, he's an investment counselor."

Caleb gave me a withering look of scorn. "Frank, honestly. An investment counselor can't murder anybody?"

What I meant, of course, was that they didn't fit my image of a murderer. Harvey Wishbone was bald and fat. "I suppose they can," I said.

"Half of them are crooks," he said. "Your money isn't safe with them. Let me tell you about Harvey Wishbone.... He cost me a fortune, with some fancy scheme he talked me into. You'll make 15% a year he said, and then the company went bankrupt. I can't tell you how much trouble that caused. Some of it was Sandra's money. But that's not what I want to talk to you about."

"OK, Caleb. Tell me what's on your mind?"

"Frank, listen," he said. "I want you to help me."

"If there's anything I can do...."

"There is. It has to do with another rumor, Frank. The rumor is that you're this fantastic amateur detective, you've solved all sorts of cases, but you're modest and so on; you won't talk about it openly, but you're going to try to find out who killed Maggie. Is this true? I know you have that reputation...."

"Me, Caleb? Oh no, good grief, I'm not a criminal lawyer, or an investigator; no thank you. It's completely out of my line. The police...."

"They're incompetent. Believe me. The ones I talked to, they seemed like utter boobs. And you're just being modest. I know what I've heard. There was that business with the book club: when the woman's husband was murdered, the woman whose house they were meeting at. Everybody says, you have a certain skill...."

"Caleb," I said, with as much firmness as I could muster. "You should know better. That I'm a great detective is... well, it's in the same category as the rumor that you and Maggie were having sex and you killed her. It's equally plausible."

He waved his hand, dismissively. "Frank, I knew you'd say that. OK, I understand, it's not what you do for a living. But you do work, well, sort of informally. Frank: at least promise me that... if this is what you're doing, that you'll keep me in the picture. Promise me, Frank. And, Frank, remember that implant we talked about, they cost a lot, and the insurance doesn't cover it...."

I stopped him cold at that point: I was not about to sell myself for a free dental implant. But in the end, I had to give way; since I had no intention of doing anything, why not humor the man? I promised Caleb I would "keep him in the picture." There would be no picture, I said to myself. Of course I was wrong.

As I was leaving, he said, rather hesitatingly: "There's another matter, Frank...."

"Another matter?"

"I told you... Sandra and I have issues. You don't know Sandra. My wife. Issues, I said. That was an understatement. She's in therapy, and she wants a divorce."

"You think it's because of the therapy?"

"I think the psychiatrist is egging her on, telling her she just married me because I was a father figure or some shit like that. But Sandra... well, she moved into the spare bedroom, we're barely speaking, she's so angry.... My home is a nightmare right now; and this on top of everything, God, it's too much."

"I'm so sorry, Caleb."

"The worst of it is... she's already hired a lawyer, about the divorce. I said, Sandra, what's the rush, think it over, maybe we can work things out.... I told her I'd do couples therapy. She said, what for? We tried it once, and you just sat there sulking. She's right. Listen, Frank. This lawyer of hers, it's a woman, Jessica Woods, and she's got a reputation, she's a ballbreaker, they're going to take me to the cleaners again. Like with Lucille. This is déjà vu all over again."

"And... where do I come in, Caleb?"

"Well, I think I need a lawyer...."

I was afraid of that. I hate divorces. They tend to be ugly. Women clients sitting in my office, crying their eyes out, talking about how awful he was, how thoughtless, all he thinks about is me me me. Or the men sitting in front me, sulking, or talking about "that bitch." I've handled a few divorces. I told Caleb, I'd prefer not to represent him in this case. I said I was booked solid, which was a lie, but that I'd refer him to Jennifer Forest, whose office is in Palo Alto. "She's tough," I said, "and knowledgeable. She's the best of the best. He nodded sheepishly and left. I don't normally turn down business. But some instinct told me to stay away from this particular affair.

I told the whole story to Celia after the dinner with Adam Finkel. It went as well as might be expected. Celia was putting away some of the leftover food. "We'll have this tomorrow, in the microwave," she said. I was hoping she wouldn't be angry because I was late—or criticize me for turning down Caleb's divorce suit. When I finished my report, she turned to me and looked me straight in the eye. Celia is a miracle of common sense and intuition. "He killed her, Frank. That's my guess. No, more than a guess. I feel it in my bones. You know, they say he has an eye for the ladies."

"You mean, he and Maggie? But she was 70 years old!"

"That doesn't stop some people, Frank. Some men will do anything for sex, you know that. But no, I don't think it's Maggie. Even though Hilda, next door, she was talking about it, and she thought it might be true. But personally, I think it's something else. Maybe she knew something about him. Some secret."

"What kind of secret?"

"Well, I wouldn't know, Frank. But remember, she was around the office, every day; if there was something funny going on, she would see it, wouldn't she?"

I had trouble imagining "something funny going on" in a dentist's office. Sex with patients, in the dentist's chair? Or some kind of fraud: telling people they had cavities, when they really didn't? Or some kind of sadistic streak, getting an erotic charge or even an orgasm out of pulling teeth? Or using the office as a front for smuggling or pushing dope? All of this seemed colossally unlikely.

"Something funny, darling?" I said. "Whatever could that be? And even so, why did he come to see me, why did he ask me to keep him informed?"

"Frank," she said, "you're so gullible. This idea that you're a great detective, which we all know is nonsense, he knows it's nonsense too. But he's flattering you, he thinks you might be mixing in, and he wants to find out what you know, when you know it. Of course he thinks it'll all come to nothing. It gives him cover, though. You won't be suspicious of him. Mark my words, my dear, he killed that woman."

"Gee, thanks," I said, mildly annoyed. "I didn't realize I was so gullible. I hope my clients never find out."

"Oh, Frank, don't be so sensitive. He doesn't know you like I do. And he's trying to throw you off the track."

"I don't know what to believe," I said.

Secretly I thought: who knows? Maybe I *will* solve the case.

Of course I had absolutely no idea how to go about doing that.

4

The next night Celia invited Chloe to dinner again. "She a relative, and she lives by herself in some room somewhere; really, we ought to see her more often," she said. "We barely know her. When I went to the dentist, I didn't even recognize her. It's a family thing. My mother couldn't stand her father, the one who gambled. Well, he's out of the picture, has been for some time. Whatever the problems were, you can't blame them on Chloe."

Of course, it didn't hurt Chloe's popularity that she was such an insider. She knew Maggie, she knew the place, she knew the whole story. Well, not the whole story—but more than I did, or most other people. And this no doubt was why we were seeing her again.

After dinner, we sat around in the living room talking. Naturally, the conversation turned to the murder. Celia asked her about Maggie, what was she like, and so on.

Chloe said, "To be honest, I didn't really know her that well. She moved her from someplace else, I think it was Ohio. Tiffany, that was the woman who worked there before, she got married, actually it was her third marriage—the new husband, he was some kind of salesman, and they moved to Atlanta, so that's why she quit; and Dr. Colegrove hired Maggie. That was before I came. Anyway, she had worked for a dentist, she said, in Cleveland. I suppose she had references. She was a really nice person, everybody liked her."

"She did seem nice," I said.

"Oh yes, the patients all liked her. She was motherly, if you know what I mean. People liked to tell her their troubles. And Dr. Colegrove, he was very fond of her, I know that. Everybody was fond of her. Well, maybe not Dr. Dobbs. But he's a real sourpuss."

Celia asked: "Dr. Dobbs?"

"That's the other dentist. He's new."

We urged Chloe on. She seemed only too happy to talk about the case. "Oh," she said, "it's so awful, why anybody should kill her. She had such a nice smile. I told you, people liked to talk to her. But she was very private, if you know what I mean. She listened to people, I think she gave people advice, but she didn't talk much about herself. Lived all alone I think. She told me once, she had been married and her husband was a terrible man. Abusive. That's the word she used, abusive. I said, do you mean, he actually hit you? She didn't want to talk about it. But then she said, yes, he had an awful temper, and he drank, it's a curse when they drink. He actually frightened me, she said. He could be sweet sometimes, she said, but later on he could be an absolute monster. She said to me, Chloe, make sure, before you get married, what kind of a man you're getting married to. Young people are impulsive, she said. She told me to be careful."

"Where does this ex-husband live?" I asked. "Could it be, he tracked her here, and... well, killed her in some sort of jealous rage?"

"I don't know where he lives. She never said. You know what I think? This mysterious Mr. Romeo, or whatever he calls himself, the one who called for an appointment but didn't show up, and he gave us a fake address and a fake phone number—I really think, this could be Maggie's ex-husband."

"And came and killed her? Is that what you think?"

"Maybe."

"I'm sure the police are checking into it, Chloe," I

said. "That's the first place they'd look, you know, the ex-husband."

"I do hope they solve it," she said. "It's getting me down. It's so strange, going to work, and...it's creepy. If I didn't need the job, I'd quit, honestly I would. You know, I won't go into that bathroom. Thank God there's another one in back, that's the one I use. And if there's somebody in that back bathroom, I swear, even if I felt like I was going to burst, I wouldn't go in the one where... where she was. Not for a million dollars."

Celia went to make coffee. It was time for coffee and dessert. Celia had come home with a fruit tart that really looked wonderful. Loaded with strawberries and blueberries. Chloe looked at it longingly. "I have to watch my diet," she said.

"Oh, it's mostly fruit," Celia said. "And blueberries, they're full of antioxidants. Very good for you."

I don't think Chloe cared about antioxidants. She was looking at the fruit tart hungrily. She agreed to take "a sliver."

"Poor Maggie liked sweets," I said. "That's what I heard."

"Oh, she did. She loved all kinds of pastry; she would go to the coffee shop next door, on her breaks. You know: one thing, I should have mentioned, about Maggie. Maybe it's just my imagination, but I thought she was acting well, funny, the last few weeks."

"Funny?"

"Well, she took a lot of breaks. I mean, she would say, Chloe dear, could you cover for me? She'd be gone for ten, fifteen minutes; I had no idea where she was going and what she was doing except, well, once... I saw her coming out of that office, you know that weird company with the funny name."

"You mean Xyloquex?"

"I think so."

"Did you ever ask her, where are you going?"

"Once I did, and she just smiled and said, nowhere in particular. I didn't think it was any of my business.... Oh, do you think this had something to do with...? Oh, Frank, I feel so awful. That poor woman."

She started to cry. I hate it when women cry. It took another "sliver" of fruit tart, antioxidants and all, to bring Chloe back to normal. I didn't bring up the murder issue again; and Chloe went home a little bit later. At Celia's insistence, she took another "sliver" along, carefully wrapped in plastic.

5

At least Chloe didn't ask me to solve the mystery myself, and she never referred to the rumors that I was some sort of great detective. She spared me that. Which is more than I can say for my next visitor, who came to the office in the morning. She was a woman in her 40's I would say, with reddish cheeks, very dark eyes, and hair that had been dyed some peculiar color I couldn't quite identify, somewhere between orange and brown. She was plump, and was wearing a black dress.

I hadn't been expecting anybody. She said: "May I come in? I need to see you."

"And you are...?"

"Helen Swift," she said. "Maggie Swift was my mother." She wiped a tear from her face.

"So sorry for your loss," I said. She wiped away another tear. I sat patiently waiting, tapping a pencil on my desk. "A lovely woman," I said.

She seemed too choked up with emotions to say anything. She said she was sorry she was making a scene and please forgive her, to which I said, of course. I wondered, was it possible she was here because she wanted me to manage her mother's estate? I doubted whether Maggie had much in the way of assets; a receptionist in a dentist's office is not a very promising client, to be perfectly honest. I can't make money on very small estates. Sometimes I do agree to manage a small estate, because I want some other business from the family. Otherwise, I have to turn it down. This can get quite embarrassing at times: people don't like to be rejected, even by a lawyer. But I have to make a living.

"She was a lovely woman," she said. "Oh, Mr. May, I just can't get over this. Mother dead! And in this awful way. I just spoke to her a few days ago. On the phone."

I made sympathetic clucking noises. Helen went on: "She was so alive. You know, I don't live around here, I live in Denver—I'm single now and I have two children, it's hard for me to come out here. I used to visit, when I was still married, but recently.... I used to call mother, every week, rain or shine, I used to say, mother, how are you? And we'd talk about things. We were both on diets. I said, mother, I inherited it from you, you're overweight, gramma was overweight, and Aunt Tina, she weighed 300 pounds, you remember? That last phone call, we talked about diets. Mother was on a grapefruit and protein diet. A lot of lean meat, and of course the grapefruit. I said, isn't that too acid for you? No, she said, it's fine. She stayed away from carbohydrates, no pasta, no potatoes, no bread; and that was hard, she said, mother always liked bread, especially rye bread. With seeds. Oh God. And of course, she said, I can't have sweets, no desserts. Don't send me that pumpkin bread you make, she said. Just think, my mother was starving herself, she was eating nothing but grapefruit, and the poor woman had only a few days to live. It's so unfair," she said, and started to cry again.

I didn't have the heart to break the news to her about the blueberry scones. Maggie was cheating, it turned out. Maybe she mostly kept to the diet, but not entirely. For all I know, Maggie died happy, with a blueberry scone nestling inside her stomach. And not a grapefruit in sight.

I felt guilty, even thinking about such things. This woman's mother was dead—killed, in fact, probably murdered. That must be very hard to take.

"She was very active in politics, mother was. She was heart and soul for the Democratic party. She did a lot of work for them. She believed in them. That's how she raised me, too. She said, Helen, just vote for the Democrats, they're for the little people. The Republicans, all they care about is big business and the billionaires. To her dying day, she was a strong Democrat. She adored Hillary Clinton. She really did. Did you know, this caused a lot of tension, in the office, where she worked? The politics, I mean. Mother told me all about it."

"Tension?"

"In the office. Mother was there for many years. When she came, there was Dr. Colegrove, and Dr. Sylvester. Lovely man, Dr. Sylvester. I met him once when I was out here. He never got married, lived with his mother. I think he was just a shy person. Mother was fond of him. This mother of his, he was very attached to her. She was a horrible creature, over 90, very demanding, deaf, and in the end, completely confused. Alzheimer's or whatever. Well, they're both dead now. I used to think, maybe mother and Dr. Sylvester would get together; they never did, and now he's dead too. Six months after his mother died. So then they hired this new dentist, Dr. Dobbs, when Dr. Sylvester died. This Dobbs, he's some sort of right-wing lunatic. That's what mother said. A right-wing lunatic. The lunatic fringe. Those were her very words. Do you think... he might be the one?"

"Dr. Dobbs?"

"The dentist, Dr. Colegrove's partner."

I knew who he was. Ryan Dobbs, D.D.S. I saw him at the dental office. I never had any professional contact with him. My teeth were exclusively with Caleb Colegrove. I told Helen I thought it didn't seem likely, I mean, a political murder. She was sobbing now, fussing with a tissue. I felt extremely uncomfortable. I said: "Mrs. Swift, I know this is a painful time for you. Is there something you would like me to do?"

She nodded, took out another tissue from her purse, and dried her eyes. Then she said: "I talked to that young woman, Chloe, she worked with my mother. She was so sweet. She told me to talk to you. She said, you're wonderful at this sort of thing."

I knew what was coming. "What sort of thing?"

"Well, not exactly detective work, but... just thinking about the issue, and maybe looking at things...."

There were those "things" again. "What things?"

"I don't know. You're here, your office is just across the street, I think you know the people who work in the building, and they say, you have a gift...."

Oh Lord, not again. Of course, I don't have a gift. And if I had one, I'd give it back to the donor immediately. I think all of these people read too many detective stories. Miss Marple sits knitting in her village, Hercule Poirot has the little gray cells, and people like Sherlock Holmes have this uncanny aptitude for deduction. He looks at a pencil or a walking stick, and he deduces God knows what. They think Frank May is in the same category. He sits in his law office, and his brain is working overtime, sifting all the clues. I suppose I should be flattered but instead it makes me uncomfortable. I can't possibly live up to this reputation. Even if I wanted to. Which I don't.

Is anybody in real life actually like those people—Sherlock Holmes, or Miss Marple? Anybody? I honestly don't think so. Oh yes, some of the detectives on TV. I mean, they get these fantastic insights, just before the program ends, and lo and behold, we know who the criminal is. And it's often a big surprise. But real life? Of course not. I suppose the police are effective, but it's because of forensic science, fingerprints, and maybe just plain dumb luck.

I won't bore you with the rest of this conversation with Helen Swift. I made the usual ineffectual protests, but they fell on deaf ears. In the end, I promised I would try to help; I don't have investigators, I don't have forensic laboratories, and I warned her not to have high hopes, but I said that I'd "do what I can." I thought inside: yes, I'll do what I can; but that's close to zero. I just couldn't flat-out refuse. I felt sorry for her. She was a nice woman, who had just lost her mother in a most awful way. I hated to operate under false pretenses, but I didn't want to hurt her feelings.

"Oh, I'm so glad," she said.

I acted as if I was already on the job, so to speak, and asked her if she could tell me anything useful, anything at all, about her mother, anything that might shed light on this awful crime.

"I didn't see much of mother in recent years.... We talked on the phone, but I haven't been out to see her in, oh, a long time. Not since we went to a cousin's wedding, that was last summer, I think, it was in Fresno, it was so terribly hot you could die. I said, mother, I promise, I'll come out more often. But I didn't. I feel guilty about that, terribly guilty, now that she's dead, poor woman. I live in Denver, I told you that; I've got small kids and I'm going through a messy divorce, my ex is behaving like a real pig, that's my excuse, and I did call every week, but still...."

"Is it possible your dad, well, was responsible for this thing?"

"My dad? He died a long time ago. Had some awful cancer."

"I thought.... I mean, somebody told me... was it your stepdad?"

"Oh, him. I never liked the man. Christopher, that was his name. I don't know why she married him. He was younger than she was. He was in his late 40's, I think, and she was a good ten years older. He was divorced. Twice, in fact. That should have been a clue. Oh, he was downright awful. Abusive, and he drank a lot. He got so nasty when he was drunk. I think he hit her once, I do believe he did, although mother wouldn't tell me the details. I said, mother, you have to get rid of him. She was crying on the phone, and I felt so helpless. I said, just leave. Well, finally she did. I think she was afraid of him, that's why it took her so long. But in the end, she did go, thank God. I have no idea where he is now.... I never wanted to see him again, and neither did mother."

"How long ago was this? I mean, when she left—when was that?"

"Four, five years ago. I don't really remember."

"Could he be.... the person who killed your mother?"

"How awful. Christopher? But why would he do that, after all this time?"

I had no idea. "Revenge? Just plain nastiness?"

"Oh, I don't know. Christopher was a terrible man, but.... Why would he wait so long? For all I know, he's got a new wife."

"Is it possible," I asked, "that there could be, well, something about money...."

"Money? Whatever do you mean?"

I really didn't want to tell her about the rumors. The blackmail rumors. "Did your mother... well, did she have enough money?"

She looked at me oddly. I realized it was a strange question, one that more or less came out of the blue. "Enough money?"

I cleared my throat. "I'm just asking.... Enough to live on?"

"She never complained.... I know mother wasn't rich, and it's very expensive around here, I can't believe the rents. I really couldn't help out, we're going through this divorce, and my youngest, Jayden, he's got asthma, but I did offer... but mother said, no, she didn't need help, she had a job, she lived pretty modestly, she drove a twelve year old Honda, and she was paying so much for her apartment—it was scandalous. But still, she had a little bit of money in the bank, and she had Social Security, and my aunt left her some money, a nest egg, if you know what I mean. And Dr. Colegrove provided benefits. I think she was okay. Can I ask, why do you bring this up, Mr. May?"

"There are so many ugly rumors. You know, when a

person dies... I mean, for instance, I've heard some talk.... Maybe blackmail...."

"Blackmail?"

"Dr. Colegrove.... That's one of the nasty rumors. That there was somebody blackmailing him. I don't know why people think so."

"My mother? Out of the question. Anybody who knew my mother...." She was on the verge of tears, groping in her purse for another Kleenex. "Oh why do people say such awful things!" The tears started flowing, and I dropped this line of questions. Which was just as well.

"Is there anything else you can tell me?"

She said, no, there wasn't. "I spoke to Dr. Colegrove. He was very sweet. Mother liked him a lot. I asked him if he had any ideas, anything at all; but he said, no, he didn't. I did ask him for a list of the people who were supposed to come in that morning, I mean, the people who had appointments with the dentist. Dr. Colegrove said yes, and he got the list from Chloe. There were only a few of them. Dr. Colegrove was supposed to leave in the afternoon, around three, there was a meeting of some dental society thing... and the other dentist, that awful man, the Republican, he had the day off, so he wasn't there at all. Anyway, I have the list. I made a copy for you."

I glanced at the list. Some of the names were familiar. I was on the list. Of course, I ruled myself out as a killer, and I hope that she did the same. Milo Feigenblatt was the next name. I knew Milo slightly. He was in the music department of the University of California at Berkeley, which is across the Bay, but he lived in San Mateo, which seemed odd to me. As it happens, his wife had a job in San Mateo, some sort of administrative job at a junior college. The list also had his address and phone number. The next name was the mysterious Hendrik Borromeo, and of course nobody knew anything about him at all. No address, no phone number. That made him some-how the number one suspect. The next name was totally unfamiliar to me: Werner Brown; the address was in Hillsborough, California, a nearby and very posh suburb. "Do you know who that man might be?" I asked.

"Oh yes," she said. "Dr. Colegrove told me, he's the CEO of some company, whose name I didn't catch, something about Quex or Quax, and Dr. Colegrove said it's right around here."

"It's the Xyloquex Corporation," I said.

There were no other names. She explained: "There was originally a Mrs. Grinder, she was scheduled for eleven o'clock, but she called in the morning, said she had a splitting headache, and she just couldn't come in."

I knew Mrs. Grinder. Cynthia Grinder. She had once been my client. She was a dreadful human being, always whining and complaining. She worked in the public library, where I'm sure everybody hated her. She was a woman of about 60. I do remember the splitting headaches, or rather, her constant failures to make appointments because of these alleged headaches. Maybe Cynthia Grinder crept in unannounced and killed the receptionist. People with headaches are capable of anything.

"Interesting list," I said, for want of anything else to say. Something about the list bothered me. I couldn't put my finger on it, for the moment.

"Oh, but I want you to talk to these people. Please. Maybe they know something."

I explained that I couldn't just call these people out of the blue... I had no official status, and what was I supposed to tell them?

"You don't have to tell them anything. I'll explain the situation to them, and they'll be happy to see you. Unless, of course, they killed my mother. Promise me you'll do this."

I had to promise, if only to get rid of her. I hated the idea of talking to "suspects." There was no particular reason to think the list included whoever killed Maggie Swift.

I suddenly realized what bothered me about the list. Stanley wasn't on the list. E. Stanley Banks, the man who actually found the dead body. I mentioned this to Helen. She said she didn't know; this was the list they gave her. "But he was there," I said. "Maybe he had a dental emergency, and called in at the last minute." As soon as I said this, I knew it was wrong. Stanley never said boo about a dental emergency. He said he had a regular appointment.

Of course, it could be nothing at all. Maybe the list was inaccurate. But I made a mental note to check this out with Stanley.

6

Celia and I spent a quiet evening at home, something I always appreciate. A couple of days later, to my surprise, Helen Swift called me at my office; she seemed quite agitated, and she said she really had to see me, was this possible?

"Sure. What's this all about?"

"I'd rather not say on the phone."

I told her I could see her in the late afternoon, I was busy until then. She agreed, and showed up at 4:30. She still seemed quite perturbed. "What's wrong?" I asked her.

"Mr. May...."

"Please call me Frank."

"Frank," she said. "I don't know what to think. I'm trying to settle mother's affairs.... She had an insurance policy and some government bonds, I knew about those. But she had some bank accounts, too; one in particular, it was at Wells Fargo, a local branch: it had a lot of money in it, more than $25,000; and I have no idea where my mother would have gotten that kind of money."

"Maybe she saved it up," I said. "She was probably very frugal. My mother was living on social security, and she didn't spend the half of it. Baffled me how she could survive, but she did."

"It's not just the amount," she said. "It's, well, the history of that account. She used to deposit a lot of money, five or ten thousand at a time; and then later on, draw out big amounts, too. Where did the money come from? And where did it go? What did she do with, I mean, thousands of dollars, when she withdrew money? I'm really upset, Frank. What was my poor dear mother up to?"

I remembered the rumors about blackmail. Could it possibly be true? And could it possibly be Maggie? A blackmailer? This sweet old lady, who worked as a receptionist? And if it was true, was this somehow connected with her death? In mystery novels, blackmail is really dangerous. For the blackmailer, that is. Gets himself or herself killed every time. Could this have been Maggie's fate?

I had already, the last time we spoke, mentioned the rumors about blackmail. Which of course Helen rejected indignantly.

"Maybe there's some sort of explanation," I said, although offhand I couldn't think of one.

"I don't know what to think," she said. "Mother was honest to a fault. I have no idea what she was doing with this money, or why. She never said a word to me about it. And she used to tell me everything," she added, and the tears began to flow. "I just can't imagine mother doing anything dishonest. You think you know people, and then, well, it turns out that you don't. This is really driving me crazy. I can't believe mother was mixed up in something. But maybe she was. This is a nightmare."

"You're sure you have no idea about the, uh, source of the money?"

"No, nothing. Oh, this is so terrible. Maybe it has something to do with drugs. I mean, all that money. But it can't be mother. She was an old lady.... You know what I think? It's Dr. Colegrove. She was so fond of him. It must have something to do with him. I don't mean blackmail. No. I just can't accept that. But something else."

Neither of us, of course, had any idea what that something else might be. The net result was a squall of uncontrollable sobs. I sat there helplessly. Finally, she left.

7

I felt a bit depressed the rest of the day. I don't know why it bothered me—the business about money. Was Maggie living two lives? My imagination ran riot. She was dealing in drugs? Seemed inconceivable. Blackmail was another absurd idea. In any event, the money seemed to flow through Maggie; it didn't end up with her. Except for the $25,000 sitting in her bank account. Maybe she was scheduled to pay that out to somebody.

I thought and thought about it. It was on my mind. That must have been obvious. Celia can read me like a book.

After dinner, she said: "Frank, what's up?"

I guess I was in the mood to talk. I told her about my conversation with Maggie's daughter, and the rash promise I made.

"Stay out of it, Frank," she said. You can count on Celia to say something sensible. She's invariably sensible. That's the trouble. Very often, the last thing you want to hear is something sensible. This occurs when the un-sensible thing is what you really want to do. Or when you don't really want to do it, but being told not to has a perverse effect. I'm not sure which one applied to this situation, but I felt that I simply couldn't follow her advice.

"Darling, I promised her."

"Promises are made to be broken. Especially foolish promises."

Nevertheless, in the morning, I called Stanley Banks. I asked, could we get together? And he agreed to have lunch. "No Chinese, Frank," he said. "Let's have a salad someplace. I get gastroesophageal reflux from Chinese food. Too greasy for me."

This was a big disappointment, but I had no choice. We went to a kind of health-food restaurant, which served a wide variety of dishes for the masochists who insist on eating there.

"So, what's up, Frank?" Stanley said, holding up a spear of asparagus.

I wasn't sure how to approach the issue, or what I was supposed to do. "Oh, nothing much, really."

"Nothing much? You call me up on the phone, you haven't done that in ten years, you want lunch, the sooner the better, and it's nothing much? Am I missing something, Frank?"

"It's this Maggie business," I said, weakly.

"What about it? I don't like to dwell on it. If I never find another corpse, it'll be too soon. What is this, Frank, morbid curiosity? Do I have to tell you again, about how I forgot to zip up my fly? Do I want my clients to think I'm on the verge of Alzheimer's? I'm trying to make a living here. I know I'm past retirement age, but I need the money. My mother's 96 years old, she's in assisted living, and it's costing me a fortune. Not to mention my daughter, she soaks up money like a sponge."

"Stanley, I know you're really sharp, intelligent, please.... It's just, well, I was wondering. I got a list of the people who were supposed to see Colegrove that morning. You know, the morning Maggie died. Funny thing, you weren't on the list."

"So what? What's this list? Is it the Holy Bible? "

I said: "Be serious, Stanley. You know what I think? I think you didn't really have an appointment. You said you did, but you didn't. Why were you there, Stanley? What were you doing there?'

"What are you, Perry Mason? What's the point of all these questions? Honestly, Frank, you're giving me heartburn."

"I just want to know."

"Well, you're not going to know, Frank. I don't have to answer your questions. I thought we were going to have a nice lunch, and instead it's the Spanish Inquisition."

"OK, OK, Stanley, forget it."

I nibbled on my broccoli, and changed the subject. I got Stanley to talk about his personal problems, which were immense—divorces, the aged mother, spoiled and difficult children, not to mention his precarious state of health. "I've got a million things wrong with me. Arthritis, diabetes, high blood pressure. It's a wonder I didn't drop dead, when I saw that dead body. Maybe I'm tougher than I think."

"You are, Stanley, you are. What an awful thing to have to go through! I feel for you. Can I ask you, though: you were there, on the scene, did you notice anything special, anything strange, anything at all that might... uh, help us out?"

"Help us out? Who's the us?"

"Nobody, Stanley, I just mean, people want to know, who did this awful thing."

"Really, Frank, I'm asking myself, what's this all about? Why are you asking me these questions? Last I knew, nobody appointed you a detective. Can I see your badge?'

"You're annoyed, Stanley. I can tell."

"I guess I am. I told you, you're giving me indigestion. Is there any earthly reason why I should answer your questions?"

"Not really, Stanley. I told you, I'm just curious."

"Oh, come on, Frank. I didn't just drop off a turnip truck. I've been around for a while, remember? And I know you've been talking to Maggie's daughter. I'd like to know, why you're mixing in."

I felt I had to tell him. I said: "The daughter... asked me to help her out."

"Help her out?"

"She had the idea, I had certain skills...."

"Skills? What on earth are you talking about, Frank? Can you tell me in plain English?"

I told him about the rumors, and of course I disclaimed them. I thought he would be annoyed. Instead, he was amused. He burst out laughing and made some comments about me and Sherlock Holmes. I felt humiliated. The broccoli on my plate stared at me in reproach. I don't like broccoli.

"You know," Stanley said, "she came to see me, too. Wanted to know if I'd handle her mother's estate."

This was something of a surprise. And a mild rejection too. Why didn't she ask me, instead of Stanley? Nobody likes to be passed over, even though, as I knew very well, I really didn't want the estate. Maggie's estate was bound to produce headaches instead of fees. "Is there actually an estate?" I asked.

"Believe it or not, there is. She has an insurance policy, which is payable to the estate, $20,000. Foolish woman, she's got the one daughter, the daughter should have been the beneficiary—but anyway, there's that. And she has some odds and ends, you know, furniture, a car, none of it very valuable. She lived in an apartment, no real estate, no stocks and bonds, but quite a bit of cash, in two separate bank accounts. One of them had about $15,000 in it, this was a checking account; and her Social Security check and her paycheck used to go directly into this account. It's at Wells Fargo. But then there's this other account, savings account, also at Wells Fargo—not that the interest amounts to anything; and it's got a lot of money in it. I mean, a lot for a person like Maggie: $25,000, to be exact. So I wondered, why did she have so much cash? And I figured, maybe she doesn't spend much. Old people are like that. Not me, though."

"And that's the whole estate?"

"Well, it's more than I expected. And I can't really make much money on it, an estate of about $60,000. No will. So everything goes to the daughter."

"Seems pretty easy."

"Well, you would think so," he said. "But actually.... There's a complication already. The other day, a lawyer called me on the phone. Somebody in Cupertino, said his name was Jerry Walden. Do you know him?"

"Never heard of him."

"Well, he's a lawyer. I guess. I looked him up. Anyway, he mentioned the savings account, you know, the one with $25,000 in it. He had the account number and everything, seemed to know all about it. Big surprise. He wanted to tell me, he said, that this money didn't really belong to Maggie. I said, what do you mean? It's in her name. He said, right, it's in her name. But the money belongs to somebody else. She was just... well, she was just holding it, on behalf of somebody else."

"Whose money was it?"

"He wouldn't say. But he claimed he had proof, or could get proof, or something like that. And I said, look, Jerry, this money's part of the estate, it's in Maggie's name, it's Maggie's money, I represent the estate, and I have a duty to protect the assets, you know that. He said, well, actually it isn't really money that belongs to the estate. I said, you expect me to hand you over $25,000, just like that, without any documentary proof, because you say it belongs to some other mysterious person, and you're not telling me who?"

"And what did he say?"

"Well, of course, he had to agree with me. He said, my client wants to remain confidential. I said, well, but he or she can't. You know that. I'm not going to transfer the money, write you a check for $25,000 without further ado, you know that, don't you? My clients would have me by the balls, they'd have the disciplinary committees all over me."

"And he said?"

"He said, yes, I know that. I realize, he said, that this is awkward, seems crazy, and I understand your position entirely. All I'm asking, right now, is that you don't do anything with that money. It's a relatively small estate, I assume; but I'm asking you to keep it open, not to distribute anything; and I will do my best to satisfy you legally that the money belongs to somebody else. But I need some time."

"And what do you make of that?"

"I don't know what to make of it. Damnedest thing I've come across, in forty years of practicing law. Well, no, it isn't. I could tell you about some really weird clients, like the guy who wanted me to put in his will that they should put his dog to sleep and bury the dog with him, right in the same coffin, for God's sake, because he knew she wouldn't want to go on living without him. A real lunatic. And the guy who wanted to leave money to erect a statue in his memory, in Golden Gate Park, and money to hire a brass band to play happy birthday, every May something, because that was his birthday. But that's neither here nor there. I'm just reporting what the guy said to me."

I had to agree: very strange. Whose money was it? And what was Maggie doing with it? And did it have something to do with... with the murder?

I found this issue so intriguing that it made me forgot my real purpose in setting up this lunch. I wanted an answer to the question that was bothering me: what was Stanley doing at Dr. Colegrove's office that morning? Why wasn't his name on the list of patients with appointments?

That was what I wanted to know; but Stanley had made it quite clear, he wasn't going to give me an answer. I decided I would ask these questions again, but later on, some other time. I wondered, why was Stanley so reticent about this question? Why was he trying to put me off the scent? As I drove home, I wondered about this issue. Stanley was, after all, a suspect. He was there that morning, he found the body, or that's what he said, so he had to be considered at least a "person of interest," as the police like to put it.

Not that he seemed to have a motive. Nothing obvious, at any rate. Maybe he killed Maggie just for the thrill of it. True, he was an old man. And a member of the bar, with nothing negative on his record, as far as I knew. But maybe he felt death was closing in on him, and why not do things finally that you never did before.

Like killing an old lady?

"Out of the question," I said to myself, as I eased my car into the driveway. "Not Stanley. Must be somebody else."

8

I did think that Stanley was holding something back. The way he dodged the issue—my issue—of why he was there in the first place.

A few days later, as it happens, I bumped into Stanley. It was right after lunch. He was sitting on a bench, in a little park not far from downtown. It was pure luck that I saw him. Normally, I go right back to the office, but I had things on my mind (not relevant here), and I decided to go for a walk. That's when I saw Stanley. His head was down, and he seemed to be either asleep or in deep thought.

"Stanley?"

He raised his head with a jerk. "Oh, Frank. You."

"In person," I said. "What are you doing here? Are you OK?"

"Had lunch with a client," he said. "And I have terrific indigestion. It feels like somebody is squeezing my stomach with some kind of torture thing. I knew I shouldn't have ordered the dessert. It was too rich for my blood."

"Sorry, Stanley," I said.

"I walked around a bit," he said. "Thought that would make things better. Didn't. I was feeling a little faint, so I sat down here."

"You did the right thing," I said.

"It's the Gerd," he said. "You know, gastroesophageal reflux disease. I don't wish it on my worst enemy. I take these pills, but do you think they work? No. Anyway, I have to be careful what I eat. Would you believe it, tomatoes are the worst. That and grapefruit."

I tried to look sympathetic.

He said: "Maggie had Gerd, we used to talk about it."

"Maggie?"

"Yes, Maggie. She was on this diet, included grapefruit. I said, Maggie, you might as well take poison. Cut out the grapefruit. I don't know if she did or she didn't."

"You were that thick with Maggie?" I asked, and sat down next to him. He was sweating. He mopped his brow with a handkerchief.

"Well, I wouldn't say thick. You know, she was a nice woman. People liked to talk to her. They confided in her. Told her all sorts of secrets. They'd ask for advice. I mean, she was motherly, people thought they could trust her. So... she knew things."

"Things? What sort of things?"

"Look, Frank. I didn't tell you about this. Maybe I should. You know, the other day, I was talking to a client, a woman—never mind her name—but she's good friends with one of your neighbors, and don't ask me who, because I forgot. Anyway: this client heard from her neighbor, how you were involved in a situation, a murder on your block, some lady's husband... and you solved it all by yourself."

"Well, that's something of an exaggeration," I said.

"But I thought: why am I hiding things from him? I should tell him. I told the police, but shouldn't I tell Frank too?"

"Told what to the police? Stanley, what are you talking about?"

"Maggie. This was quite a while back. Maybe a couple of years, I can't remember exactly. I was there in the office, getting my teeth cleaned. Maggie said she wanted to speak to me. I got done and she took me aside, she said, I'm on break now, and we went next door—you know the coffee shop, that place where Felicity works, you know it. She said, I've got a question I want to ask you, you're a lawyer, right? I said, yes, OK, let me have it. Then she said, what if you knew that somebody had killed somebody else, and you don't go to the police, is that a crime?"

I said: "Wow."

"That's the way I felt. I said, Maggie: what is this all about? You knew that somebody killed somebody else?"

"And what did she say?"

"Well, she seemed to back off. She said, I didn't say I knew. I said, 'what if somebody knew?' But I asked her, well, why are you asking me this thing, Maggie? Is it because of some book you read? Or you saw some show on TV?"

"And what did she say?"

"Well, for a while she didn't say anything. The waitress came over, you know, Felicity, and she said something to Maggie, we've got these blueberry scones, or something like that. They chatted for a minute or two, and then she went away... Maggie was quiet again, and I thought, well, that's that. But then she said: No, it's not something I read about, and it's not some movie or TV show, it's real. And it's bothering me."

"And then what happened?"

"Well," Stanley said. "I was really curious, you can imagine. So I said, it's hard to say, Maggie. It all depends. But who are you talking about?"

"What did she say?"

"She said, I can't do that. I can't tell you. I'm not going to tell. Not ever. But I just wanted to know, am I committing a crime myself, if I don't tell what I know? OK, I said, I understand. But let me ask you one thing. Are you sure, absolutely sure, 100% positive, that this person really did kill somebody? And she said, yes I'm sure. I didn't see him; but he told me. He was upset, and he told me."

"And she actually said him, Stanley? Are you sure of that? So it was a man she was talking about?"

"Yes. She said: him."

"So what does it mean, Stanley? You think she was telling the truth?"

He said: "Why would she lie? She was troubled. She was worried. I think she was telling the truth. She knew somebody's secret. And maybe... that's why she died."

"But when was this, Stanley? That's important."

"I know it is. I told you, I can't remember. It wasn't recently. It was maybe a couple of years ago. Maybe more. Maybe less. Listen, Frank, I'm not as young as I used to be. I have these senior moments, you know what I'm talking about? The other day, I just couldn't remember the name of my tax guy. Been going to him for years. A real character. Lives in a house in San Francisco, he's got six cats, the whole place is full of those disgusting boxes, you know, kitty litter. Couldn't remember his name for the life of me. So don't ask when this was. It was a while ago. I honestly couldn't say how long."

"But now... you think, she knew something, and maybe that person, the one who killed somebody, that person got scared, suddenly, for whatever reason... and he killed her?"

"What do you think, Frank? It's possible. Or it could be nothing at all. No connection. I mean: if this guy killed somebody, and she knew about it, and then he decided she had to go, why did he wait so long? Did something happen?"

I shrugged my shoulders. "I have no idea, Stanley."

He got up off the bench. "You know, I'm feeling better. I should get back to the office."

I said: "Don't go yet. You told this to the police?"

"I did. I don't think they thought much about it. I mean, what is it? I don't have a name, I don't have anything. I don't even remember when this happened. I think they just filed it away and forgot about it, if you know what I mean. Thought of me as a harmless crank. You know, when there's some sort of big crime, or somebody's kidnapped, every nut in the county writes in or calls and puts in their two cents. I think they put me in that category. But you, Frank... I think you'll take it seriously. Now I really got to go."

I walked around the park a little bit more. I was no better off than the police. I had no way of knowing how seriously to take this—and if I did take it seriously, which I was in fact inclined to do, there was nothing much I could do by way of follow-up. But it did at least suggest a motive: a reason why somebody might want to kill Maggie. But why now? Maybe because she was black-mailing somebody. That mysterious bank account.

I laughed inside at the idea of me, Frank May, the great detective. In fact, right now, the great detective was totally clueless. About everything.

9

The next name on the list of patients with appointments to see Dr. Colegrove, that fatal morning, was one Milo Feigenblatt. I checked him out on Google; he also had a brief entry in Wikipedia. He was a composer, it seemed. Prominent in "avant-garde" music, whatever that meant. He was a professor at Berkeley, in the music department, which, of course, is on the other side of the Bay, across the Bay Bridge. But he lived on this side, and so it was only natural he'd use a local dentist.

I had to find some excuse to talk to him. I couldn't really think of any... so I decided to tell him the truth. I called him at his office. I got him right away (this rarely happens these days), and was struck by how cheerful he sounded. Even the way he said hello seemed to label him as somebody who was... well, cheerful.

I said my name was Frank May, and I started to stutter out something inane, but he interrupted me. "You don't need to explain. I know why you want to talk to me; it's about poor Maggie. Her daughter called me and said you were interviewing all the suspects. I said, cool! I've never been a suspect. I actually love the idea. Me, a suspect. I'm 45 years old, and I've never been a suspect. About anything. I told Zelda—she's my wife—hey, honey, I'm a suspect. You're a private detective, right?"

"Mr. Feigenblatt, or should I say Dr. Feigenblatt?"

"Just call me Milo. I'm a very informal guy. And I've never met a real private detective before. I've been married four times, and my second wife, Zadie, she got suspicious, she wanted to check up on me, and I thought she was going to hire a detective. But she didn't—and a good thing, too, because she would have found things out I didn't want her to know. She changed her mind because she had a boyfriend herself. Can I call you Frank? How long have you been in the business?"

"Milo: first of all, yes, you can call me Frank. Second, I'm not a private detective. I'm not any detective at all. I'm just a lawyer. I'm not really working on this, uh, case. I'm just doing Helen Swift a favor. That's Maggie's daughter. And, really, I don't consider you a suspect. I mean, I just told her I'd interview the patients, the ones that were supposed to be there that morning, to see if they have anything to contribute... I mean, to see if they know anything."

"Well, whatever. I get it. You're looking for clues. The police don't seem to think I'm a suspect, either, by the way. They asked a few dumb questions, that's all. But of course they're incompetent. So: when do you want to see me?"

We fixed on a time; and Milo appeared on the dot. It was an unusually hot day, by northern California standards. Tourists often think we're the tropics, and of course we're not. San Francisco can be downright cold and foggy and nasty. My part of the peninsula is a lot better. It's always cool at night, and even when the daytime temperature is broiling, it's nice and pleasant in the shade. Anyway, this was a very hot day. Milo sat down heavily, and mopped his forehead with a handkerchief.

He was very short, quite bald except for a few wisps of hair which he arranged here and there on his skull, and he had a body build best described as pudgy. He was wearing blue jeans and an orange T-shirt, with two music clefs in front and the words Make Mine Music. He seemed to have trouble sitting still. He fidgeted in his chair... but it seemed less about nervousness than just sheer animal energy. He had an irresistible smile. "So, you're a lawyer,

Frank."

"Guilty as charged."

We shook hands. His palm was sweaty but he had a good grip. "I had an uncle once who was a lawyer. My father's brother, Stewart. He was an ambulance chaser, if you want to know the truth. Wanted me to follow in his footsteps. We'll be partners, he said, Feigenblatt and Feigenblatt. The money's good, he said. I have to tell you, my father was dead already, and Uncle Stewart was sort of a father substitute. Anyway, I didn't want to be a lawyer. I wanted music, music, music. I always loved music. I'm in the music department at Berkeley. I teach piano and composition. Are you a music lover?"

"I guess. Isn't everybody?"

"I wouldn't say that. Everybody thinks they like music. The kids, they listen, but they don't hear anything. They go around with things in their ear, they're plugged in, 24/7. But do they really hear? Do they know what music really is? That's the question. By the way, do *you* know, Frank? I mean, do you know what music really is?"

I was not about to say I knew what music really was. Certainly not in front of a faculty member of the Berkeley music department. "Not really, Milo."

"People say: ah, that's music. And they say: ooh, that's noise. Music and noise. But do we actually know the difference? I'm a professor, I like to ask hard questions, Frank. I like to explore boundaries, you know, boundary lines. That's the Berkeley way. Hey, Frank, you're a lawyer: do you like to push the envelope, if you know what I mean? In your work?"

I said nothing. I don't think my clients want their envelopes pushed. But Milo didn't wait for an answer; he went right on. "We've got music all around us, you know? Hey, maybe you don't recognize it. You say, well, it's noise, it's not music, somebody banging on a garbage can, you know? But what makes it noise instead of music? I go into class, the students are sitting there, there's a piano in the corner of the room—but I don't go near it. Instead, I take a hammer out of my desk and I start hitting the desk. I say, is that music or is it noise? They say, it's noise. Then I say, but if I hit a drum, that's music? What's the difference? Do you get the idea, Frank?"

I told him I did. Actually, I didn't.

"I'm pushing their envelope, Frank," he said. "There's this piece I wrote. I call it 'Untitled.' That's right: the title is 'Untitled.' I like paradoxes. Anyway, it calls for a full orchestra, the works, strings, woodwinds, brass, percussion. The players come on stage, one at a time. There's nothing written out for them. They play whatever they want: scales, random notes, tunes, whatever they like. It makes a big, glorious mish-mash, like the way the orchestra sounds when it's tuning up. Then, as soon as the last player gets on stage, they start leaving, one by one. I give them specific directions: who leaves and when. The violas go first, then the French horns, and so on. They have to go in the order I tell them to; it's all written out. The last three on stage are a piccolo player and a tuba and a percussionist. They're supposed to play as loud as they can: you know, the contrast. The piccolo, it's high and shrill, and the tuba, it's deep and resonant, very low. The third guy, he bangs the drum, he makes crashing noises on the cymbals, whatever he wants. Then he goes. So only two are left, the piccolo and the tuba. The piccolo player has to be a man, and a woman plays the tuba. Paradoxical, right? Then the two of them embrace, they kiss each other, passionately I hope; anyway, it's a symbolic act. And then they walk off. Then it's silence."

I wondered what the audience would think of this masterpiece. I made no comment. It didn't matter. Obviously, Milo loved to talk.

"I mean, there are these dichotomies," Milo said. "Music and noise. Silence and sound. Man and woman. I want to challenge these dichotomies, you know? I want people to think: what is silence, and what is sound. I think that's important, don't you?"

"Man and woman?"

"Another dichotomy," he said. "I used to talk to Dr. Colegrove about this. He liked music, anyway, he said he did. Used to go to the symphony, he said. While he was drilling my teeth, he was playing Mozart in the background, I think maybe he had some sort of music service. Soothing, he said. I said, maybe you should try something else, maybe loud noise, drums, or the noise of a jet airplane. See what that would do for your patients."

"What did he say?"

"He said, oh great, just what I need. If I played that noise, it would send people across the street, to Dr. Flansbaum. He didn't get the point. Well, I expected that. I said, Dr. Colegrove, I'm going to put you into music. How so, he asked me. I said, I'm writing a concerto for dentist and orchestra. You like Mozart: well, here's the orchestra sitting on the stage, playing a Mozart symphony, maybe something he wrote when he was twelve years old. I'm not sure yet what they're playing. Maybe I'll have them play two symphonies by Mozart, both at the same time; that would be a kick. And in front of the conductor, there's a dentist, and he's got a patient, sitting in the chair, and he's using a noisy, high-power drill, and he's drilling a patient's teeth. I mean, my trips to Dr. Colegrove, they gave me this idea. You think this is crazy? The Oakland symphony, they played one of my pieces last year, it was a big success. It was a kind of sequel to my Untitled piece. I called it, Symphony No. 6. That's a joke. There's no symphony 1, 2, 3, 4, 5. Anyway, the orchestra came in, they took out their instruments, and they started talking to each other—it wasn't scripted, I just said, talk about anything, you and the guy next to you; talk about the weather, any old thing. And then, after five minutes, they all left the stage, except the double bassoon player, and he went to the front of the stage and said to the audience, now let's have a big round of applause. What do you think of that, Frank?"

"You want my honest opinion? I think I'd ask for my

money back," I said. "After all, I came to hear music, not musicians talking about the weather."

"Hey, I don't blame you for feeling that way," Milo said. "That's the point. I wanted to challenge people, you know, mix them up, make them think. Pushing the envelope. Can't conversation be music? Anyway, there's a guy on the board of the Oakland symphony, he loved it. Made a zillion dollars with a hedge fund, whatever that is. He's behind me 100%. I'll let them have the world's premiere of my dentist symphony. I wanted Dr. Colegrove to be the dentist, the one on stage, but he said, no thank you. Maybe his young associate would do it, Dobbs. Maybe that's a better idea. And, oh yes, I want the dentist to be naked."

I was speechless.

"You're investigating the murder, aren't you? That's the point of this interview, isn't it? I mean, that poor woman, Maggie...."

"No, really, I'm not investigating," I said, "believe me. I promised to find out a few things, the daughter, Maggie's daughter, she talked to me, and I couldn't say no. But honestly, I don't think I can get anywhere, really. The police... I mean, they have laboratories, they have all the facilities, and they can get warrants, subpoenas, they can do all of those things, things I can't do. And anyway, it's their day job, it isn't mine, if you know what I mean."

"Oh, but if you have brains, you'll be way ahead of the police. They can't think outside of the box. I have a feeling, you're going to be successful. Last night, we ate in a Chinese restaurant, me and Zelda...."

"Excuse me?"

"Chinese restaurant. I love Chinese food. This was delicious. I think the Chinese are going to rule the world. We're history, this country. Look at our food. I mean the native food, if you can call it that. Hamburgers, meat loaf. White bread. Hostess cupcakes. Anyway, I got this marvelous fortune cookie. It said, you will meet a man who solves riddles. That must be you."

"Milo," I said, "I don't have your faith in fortune cookies. And I haven't solved a riddle since high school."

"There's a first time for everything. Meanwhile, go on with it. I love being a suspect."

I didn't know what to say. "Well, as I told you, you're not really a suspect. I mean, why should you kill Maggie? The only thing is, you had an appointment with Dr. Colegrove...."

"But I never kept it. When I got there, there were police, and a big crowd, and I found out what had happened. Such a pity. She was a sweet lady. I used to talk to her, while I was waiting for the doctor."

"I knew her too. This is awful."

"A tragedy," he said. "And also, it was clumsy, crude. You know, when you're a musician, you think a lot about what we mean when we call something beautiful. There's another dichotomy for you. What's beautiful, and what's ugly? In a way, they're much the same, don't you think? It's how you look at things. Take Las Vegas. You think it's kitsch, most people do. Tasteless. Ugly. Well, not the millions of people who go there. Think of that. Those people, they think it's beautiful."

I hadn't been to Las Vegas in years. I went there on business a while back. Oddly enough, that trip also concerned a murder... but I won't bore you with that story right now. I couldn't stand the place. All those people at the slot machines, looking like zombies. I lost $10 and decided: enough is enough.

"You can do anything artistically," he said. "Like the way you eat. You know, the way you handle a knife and fork. The way you have sex. Some people grunt and groan; and they sweat a lot. That's not beautiful. The point is: you can make anything beautiful. Even murder."

"Murder?"

"This one was totally disgusting. Smashing her head, blood all over the place. And putting the body in a toilet stall. That's crude. And no shoes. They took her shoes off. Why? Anyway, the whole thing, it was truly offensive. Is it wrong for me to say this? Murder can be artistic, you know? That doesn't make it right. It's definitely not a nice thing to do, after all, the victim is dead, and some people might miss him. Or her. I wouldn't want to kill anybody. Well, maybe a few people. I knew an oboist once, I wanted to kill him. I didn't though. But if I had, I would have tried to make it... beautiful. You know?"

I was imagining the next magnum opus by Milo Feigenblatt: concerto for murderer and orchestra. They're playing Mozart in the background, the conductor is waving his baton, the violins are scraping away, and in front of the stage, somebody is getting strangled. The victim makes all sort of gurgling and gasping noises. Would Milo love that or what?

These were awful thoughts, and I dismissed them. Even Milo would never do such a thing. The naked dentist was bad enough. Was Milo serious about this talk—an artistic murder? He seemed so sweet, so goofy, so good-natured; mildly off-key, to use a music phrase. But I couldn't conceive of him as a murderer.

And certainly, why would he kill Maggie? No motive, for one thing. And, if you believed him, he would never do so sloppy and ugly a job. Or did he tell me that story about beautiful murders just to throw me off the scent?

What on earth am I thinking?

I asked him a few canned questions: had he seen anything strange or unusual (he hadn't)? Did he have any thoughts about the case (he didn't)? I quickly ran out of questions.

"I didn't give you much of anything," he said. "I knew that would happen. But I want you to talk to Zelda. My wife, Zelda. She's going to be way more help. Zelda. She's a suspect too, didn't you know that?

"She is?"

"She was supposed to meet me after I got done with

the dentist. So she was in the neighborhood. She doesn't have an alibi."

"Does she need an alibi?"

"Don't we all," he said.

10

I was beginning to get a bit impatient. I had work to do after all. Milo was an endless stream of words. Now he was going on about his wife, Zelda.

"She was one of Dr. Colegrove's patients. Maybe that's one place to look. Disgruntled patients. These lunatics, the ones who shoot up post offices and places, they're always disgruntled people, ex-employees, you know? So this disgruntled patient, he might have come, he had a wisdom tooth pulled or root canal, and it unhinged him, so he decided to kill the doctor. But Maggie was in the way, and he killed her instead. I mentioned this theory to Zelda."

"And what did she think?"

"Not much. Did you know, I met her at Dr. Colegrove's. Believe it or not, Maggie introduced her to me. Zelda was waiting to have her teeth cleaned. Maggie was there, as usual. I came in half an hour late; I was supposed to come at 3:00, I got there at 3:30 or so. I don't remember why. Fate. Karma. Maggie said, Milo, you're late, and this woman is supposed to have her teeth cleaned at 3:30. And I looked at her. She was very very tall... I love that. I said to Maggie, introduce her to me. And then I heard her name: Zelda. I fell in love, immediately. It was the letter Z that did it. So mysterious, so... fraught, if you know what I mean. Zelda Valdez. Not just one Z: but two of them. And the last name, it's got all the letters of Zelda in it, plus a V. I thought: this is karma.

This woman has to be mine. And she was everything I always wanted in a woman. Frank, you'll love her. She'll be here soon."

"Here?"

"She's coming here, to pick me up. She's really wonderful. You'll be amazed."

As if on cue, there was a knock on the door, and in came Zelda. She was a strikingly tall woman—over 6 feet tall, I'd say; maybe a bit more. Very tall, and very thin, with a hooked nose, a pointy chin, and extremely black hair. She looked like one of the witches in *The Wizard of Oz*. Milo stood on tiptoes to give her a friendly peck on the cheek. They made an odd couple. "This is my Zelda," he said. "Isn't she something?"

I agreed of course. Everybody is at least "something."

"It was love at first sight," he said. "I told you how we met. Actually, I was still married to my third wife, at the time. But once I saw Zelda, I just knew it was all over with my third wife, Zoe. She was history. When I went home that day, after I arranged to see Zelda for dinner, I confronted Zoe: I said, this might or might not be a surprise, but I can't be with you anymore. This just isn't working."

I couldn't help asking: "You've been married four times?"

"So far," he said. "But this one will last."

"Oh Milo," she said, pinching his cheek.

"My first wife was very skinny, all bones, you know? Tall and skinny. I think she was borderline anorexic. Me, I love to eat, but I don't like fat women. I mean, they have a right to be fat, but I don't feel attracted to them. My first wife was named Zenobia. She was a good woman, but very depressed all the time. I guess I didn't help. Don't get me wrong. I tried; I really wanted to make a go of it. Then she started eating and eating. She must have gained a hundred pounds. I'm not saying that's what killed the marriage, but it was a definite factor."

Zelda pinched his cheek again. "I was married before, myself," she said. "He was a furrier, named Martin Moskowitz. I divorced him when I joined an animal rights group. I couldn't live with a man who made his money off dead animals. Now I have Milo. I'm a lucky woman, I am. What a guy! I'm putting him in my new book. As the hero."

"She writes romance novels," Milo said.

Zelda added, "You know, I was also a patient of Dr. Colegrove, somebody recommended him. I didn't like my last dentist. He was a Republican. Before that, I had Dr. Flansbaum but the chemistry was wrong. I switched to Dr. Colegrove. The last time I went to him, it was, oh, about two months ago. I had a problem with a wisdom tooth. He wanted to take it out. I said, no thank you. I hate extractions. I said, fix it, but don't take it out. It's part of me. Dr. Colegrove was very understanding. I don't think Flansbaum would have had the same attitude. So I really like Dr. Colegrove. I'm putting him in my book, too. I mean, there's no dentist in the book, but I have to visualize people—when I write about them, I have to think of somebody I know, their face, their body, otherwise, I just can't do it."

Milo gave her another tiptoe kiss.

"I used to write about pirates," she said. "I thought, pirates are really sexy: dangerously virile. But I think that's been done to death. My last book didn't sell that well. The publisher is getting nervous. That book, it had an exotic setting, Pacific Islands, you know, palm trees, coconuts, and happy natives. And then there came this British vessel, and the captain, he's not young, he's a cruel, selfish man—actually, he's Dr. Colegrove, not that Dr. Colegrove is cruel, but he looks like Dr. Colegrove, I describe him to look like Dr. Colegrove. This is the captain, and he has this terribly young and beautiful wife, and the ship has to stay on the island for a while, needs repairs—I had to ask somebody for the technical stuff, you know, about eighteenth century ships. Anyway, the wife,

Sophia, well, she falls desperately in love with the son of the island chief, who's very handsome, very young, just barely old enough to do it, you know, with coffee-colored skin, and so on. He was promised to the daughter of another chief on the island, but Sophia takes his virginity, in the moonlight, by a lagoon, you know, it's a wonderful scene; and Sophia gets pregnant, and it all ends tragically. I liked it, but the public didn't. I'm not sure why."

"People want trash," Milo said. "But it has to be the right trash."

"I thought of doing vampires," Zelda said. "Vampires are totally in. I had a long talk with Maggie about vampires, once. Do you think that's relevant? I don't think she was really interested, but she pretended. I had to wait a long time in the office that particular day; Dr. Colegrove had an emergency to deal with. You know, there really are such things as vampire bats. In Central America. Little things. They sneak up on you, and make a slit with their long teeth, then they lap up the blood with their little tongues. Can you imagine? You're asleep and this creature is sucking your blood."

"I told her, don't do vampires," Milo said. "The next big thing is zombies."

"I can do zombies," she said, "but maybe there's room for one more book about vampires. I know, maybe people have had enough, that twilight thing was all the rage, a handsome young vampire in love with a high school girl, in some town in Oregon. Or was it Idaho? They had werewolves too in that book. Made a fortune. Anyway, if I do vampires, I'm going to change the vampire's sex. It'll be a beautiful young woman. I mean, she looks young, of course she's six hundred years old; she was born in Transylvania, and the original Dracula turned her into a vampire. She lives exclusively off the blood of young men, you know, real studs. I call her Zelda, isn't that a kick? Anyway, she's extremely sexy, she finds these men, they think they're seducing her, and she bites them and sucks their blood. Very sexual, of course. But then so was the original Dracula. I mean, if you remember the story, he only preys on young virgins. Made you wonder, why only women? I mean, blood is blood."

She didn't really give me a breathing space to reply, so I suppose the question was rhetorical. Zelda went on: "Well, anyway, my vampire, my Zelda, she kills these men, she doesn't care—she's a vampire after all. She doesn't want to kill them, but she sort of goes overboard at times, and drinks gallons of blood, and they die. But then she falls in love with a young artist, very sweet, very delicate young man, very gentle, it's Paris, just after the French Revolution, very exciting time—lots of background in the book, you know, she saves him from the guillotine—anyway, she's madly in love with Armand, that's his name, and he has such soulful eyes. He's attracted to her, and they have sex, in his artist's studio, you know, very Bohemian, they're all naked in bed together and she bites him. He loses consciousness and she realizes: oh, I love him so! I can't do this to him. I want him to live, and be mine, etc. But he's an aristocrat, and he's doomed to go to the guillotine, she can't keep on saving him, and the only way she can manage, is to turn him into a vampire, then he'll be immortal. Isn't that a kick?"

Here too I think I was not really expected to answer. Zelda went roaring on: "Of course, if his head is chopped off, I was wondering, can even a vampire survive? Do they grow a new head? I have to check on this. Anyway, later on in the story, she's in love again, the young French guy left her, he discovered he was gay, and he ran off with another vampire, a handsome man from Brazil. And now she's madly in love with another artist, she has a thing for artists... and she wants to be normal, to be human, but how can you do that? She finds out, there's a way to do it, it's hard, like getting rid of a tattoo; there's a secret elixir, there's only a little bit of this stuff in the world, and it's owned by a small, tiny company, secret company. They demand millions of dollars and they want her to commit crimes. That's the plot. Unless she kills all these people, they won't give her the elixir. But she's absolutely besotted with this man, his name is Felix, and she's desperate to have him. And she doesn't want to turn him into a vampire."

"She wanted to call the company that makes the elixir Xyloquex," Milo said, "like that company around here. I told her, Zelda my dear, you're asking for a lawsuit. So she changed the name."

"I did," she said, "I call the company Quetzalfax. But really, I don't want to bore you by talking about my books. I have serious business. I want to talk about that company. Xyloquex. I mean, what kind of a business is it? Nobody seems to know. Do you know, Frank?"

I had to confess I had no idea.

"For all you know, it's a secret coven, they have satanic practices, or they're vampires. I don't really mean that. I'm joking. Actually, I saw the president of the company once.... Oh dear, I'm rambling now. But I thought of vampires. You know, poor Maggie, and there was blood everywhere...."

"Zelda my sweet," Milo said, "Frank is a busy man. He has clients. You don't honestly think that a vampire killed Maggie. Or that this company is actually a den of vampires."

"No, honeybun, of course I don't. But I do think there's a connection. I mean, between Dr. Colegrove's office and that company. Last time I had an appointment here—and I go every three months. Like clockwork. I love going to the dentist. Milo doesn't."

"No, sweetie, I don't."

"Milo can be so ordinary," she said, turning to me. "Oh, not about music... but about dentists and things. Me, I think there's something very romantic, erotic even, about going to the dentist. You know, the white coat, the whole atmosphere, the drilling, the way those devices act, the way they look, the way they vibrate. But never mind.

Anyway, I had this appointment. I came in early, I was just outside the office, and then this woman, Charlotte—she works there, you know, she's a dental assistant—I see her coming out of the office, the Xyloquex office, and I wondered, now what was she doing there? And I went into the dentist's office, I waited a bit, then I had my teeth cleaned, and it was Charlotte who did it. And I said, Charlotte, what were up to, I just saw you, you were over there at the Xyloquex company, and she said, oh no, you must be mistaken, I've been here all the time. Well, I said, do you have an identical twin? Because I was sure it was you. She said, of course I don't have an identical twin, but you must have made a mistake. It wasn't me."

"You think she was lying?"

"Well, she must have been. It was absolutely her."

"But sweetie," Milo said. "That's really odd. When I had my last appointment, I saw somebody coming out of that office, the Xyloquex office... but it wasn't Charlotte, it was Maggie. She looked upset. We went into the office, I mean, the dentist's office, the two of us. But I didn't ask her, what were you doing there? I mean, it was none of my business."

"You see," Zelda said. "There's something funny going on with that company. Maybe the people in the company, maybe they were spying on Dr. Colegrove, they paid people off to spy on him. Charlotte, and maybe Maggie too."

"You think so? I don't think it's likely," I said. But I was intrigued by this conversation. After all, Maggie had some mysterious source of money: could it come from the Xyloquex Corporation?

"Maybe they're a front for the CIA," Zelda said. "Like that terrible company, Blackstone or Sparrowhawk or whatever it was called, mercenaries, making trouble all over Africa and things like that. I can't see why they would be concerned with Dr. Colegrove, but who knows? Or maybe it's his new partner, Dr. Dobbs. What do you think, Frank?"

"It sounds farfetched, Zelda. Really," I said.

She said: "I think Charlotte was involved. Maggie found out. I think she knew something, something she wasn't supposed to know. These people are utterly ruthless, aren't they? I mean, the CIA, and all those other companies, the ones they hire. They can get away with anything; they have these secret places, billions of dollars, and who knows what they're up to? And here's this company, Xyloquex, nobody seems to know what they do. Maybe it's something to do with drones. You know, they could be sitting at computers, they have the controls, they're guiding the drones. Maybe the drones are watching us. Did you know they have little teeny drones, now? You think there's a bee buzzing around your head... but it's really a tiny drone, spying on you."

"Zelda," I said. "You don't really expect me to launch some sort of investigation of this company, this Xyloquex place. I admit, I can't imagine why Maggie or Charlotte would visit the place. I can't ask Maggie, she's dead; and there's no point talking to Charlotte, because, as you said, she just denies the whole thing."

"Maybe Dr. Colegrove works for the CIA," Milo said. "How's that for a theory? Maggie and Charlotte both worked for him. He sends them over there to give their reports."

"Reports?" I asked. "On what?"

"He's a dentist," Zelda said. "Dentists have access to people's teeth. Here's what I think. The CIA is looking for somebody, somebody very dangerous. I'm going to use this in my next novel. It just popped into my head, but it's a wonderful idea. This dangerous person, he's a jihadist, he's from Al Qaeda, I'll give him an Arab name, Abdul or Mohammed or something... anyway, he's gone underground, he's in deep cover, he had plastic surgery done, and they even altered his fingerprints; but there's always the dental records. Dental records are amazing. So the CIA, they recruit this dentist, because they know Abdul so and so is in this area, but they can't find him, except, they can use the dental records. That's the plot device. Just a novel. But you know, Frank, truth is stranger than fiction."

"Sometimes," I said. "And sometimes not."

"You're not serious, sweetie pie, are you?" Milo asked. "About the dental records?"

"Half serious, honey," she said. "Maybe it's all true. Maybe that's what Dr. Colegrove is all about. Maggie was working for him, and now she's dead, Abdul so and so killed her... maybe Charlotte is next, except she's so frightened; the doctor is too, so they have to keep their mouths tightly shut."

"Sweetie, I love you, you're ingenious," Milo said.

"You think so? You're such an angel," she said. "And I'm really turned on by this whole affair. Poor Maggie! She's dead and gone, and we're like vultures, if you know what I mean. I intend to get to the bottom of this. We'll work together, Frank. We'll put our heads together. Two heads are better than one."

I protested weakly but it was no use, which didn't surprise me. Zelda was off and running. Theories poured out of her.

She could have gone on all afternoon, and no doubt she would have. Fortunately, I had to meet a client, and so I gently but firmly nudged them toward the door.

11

Of course, all this talk about Xyloquex was absurd. Still, there was something definitely odd about that company. For example: I tried to find out what they did, using that old and trusty method, Googling them. I found nothing. They had no website. Now that really was strange. A business nowadays without a website? To the best of my knowledge, even a hot dog stand is likely to have a website. But not Xyloquex.

I was thinking about what to do next, the morning after this visit. Should I try to solve the mystery of the Xyloquex company? But how?

I still had a couple of people to interview. I realized now that Maggie's daughter was laying the groundwork, calling people, getting them to agree to an interview. At least I wouldn't have to mumble some embarrassing white lies. I felt foolish in this role as The Great Detective, but deep down, honestly, I must have enjoyed it.

I kept thinking, too, about the blackmail issue. Maggie told Stanley that she knew about a murder. And then she had some mysterious source of money. A bank account with $25,000. All right, that's not millions—and here in Silicon Valley, you don't count as rich unless you're worth at least a billion. But still, for a receptionist, this was serious money.

Maggie: was she the key? I suppose she was—she was the victim, after all. Everybody said she was sweet and wonderful, and I'm sure she was. At least she seemed that way: a nice, generous, friendly woman, a woman people liked to confide in. A quiet, elderly woman, with a taste for blueberry scones, in violation of her diet; and yet... something just didn't jibe....

And then there was Stanley. Why was he there that morning? It wasn't actually for dental work; I was convinced of that. He had come to see somebody. Dr. Colegrove? Maggie? Or somebody else? But who else was there that morning? As far as I knew, only Estelle, the dental assistant.

This particular morning, I hadn't expected to see any clients. I came to the office early; I had plenty of work to do, and I plunged into it. At about ten o'clock I had a phone call, just as I was about to take a coffee break. The voice on the other end identified itself as Dr. Ryan Dobbs. "I'm Dr. Colegrove's partner," he said. He also said that he would like to see me, if that was possible. Well, it was certainly possible. We made an arrangement for the late afternoon. "I see patients until five, then I'll come over," he said.

Dobbs appeared in my office shortly after five. He was young—about thirty, I would guess. He had pale blue eyes, and blonde hair—it was the color you would describe as dirty blond, but there was nothing dirty looking about Ryan Dobbs. His hair was carefully combed, and he was immaculately dressed in a business suit, shirt, and tie. There was something about him that seemed—I don't know quite how to put it—unfriendly. To me and to all of humanity. Or was I acting on the basis of prejudice? I remember hearing that he was a flaming right-winger. I live in San Mateo. Everybody on my block—well, basically, everybody for miles around—votes Democratic. This is California. It's not the Bible Belt, it's not Idaho, believe me. And Maggie, as I recalled, was a downright party activist. There are Dobbses in California, Tea Party types, but they're a distinct minority. Apparently, he and Maggie never got along... at least so I was told.

Dobbs introduced himself, and then got right to the point. I had assumed I owed this visit to Helen Swift, but it turned out I was wrong. He had something entirely different in mind. "Colegrove recommended you. I told him, I think I need a lawyer. I've never used lawyers. I'll be frank with you: I avoid lawyers. I consider them parasites. Bottom feeders. All these wretched lawsuits, they're sucking the blood out of the free enterprise system. They stir up trouble; it's a kind of blackmail. Take that lawsuit against McDonald's, you know, this greedy old lady, she poured hot coffee on herself, just careless, then she wants millions of dollars from the company. An absolute disgrace. I'm telling you this, so you should know: I'm not a fan of the profession. But I know there are times when they're useful. And I need your advice."

I didn't appreciate hearing myself described as a bloodsucking parasite or a bottom feeder. Who likes bottom feeders? Halibut, sole, and flounder are the only bottom feeders people actually like. And who needed that diatribe against lawyers? How would he feel if I poured out a bucket of venom about dentists? Dobbs was off on the wrong foot, as far as I was concerned. But a client is a client after all. Dentists, I suppose, make good money. I don't ask people what their politics are when they come to me. I give them advice, try to help them; and then take their money. "What sort of advice do you need?"

"Well," he said, "it all started at this dental convention, in Portland, Oregon. Both of us went: I went, and Colegrove went. I don't mean we went together. I mean, we were both there, at the meeting. I don't usually go to those conventions, they're mob scenes, a waste of time and money. But this time they invited me, I was going to give a talk on holistic dentistry, it's something I've gotten very interested in. I won't bore you with details. Normally I stay away from my fellow dentists. I don't much like them."

That made two professions he despised, one of them his own. I wonder what he felt about architects, accountants, and chiropractors.

"You don't like dentists?" I said, just to say something.

"Do you like them?" he said. "They're mostly narrow-minded idiots. Not that that makes them special. Most people are narrow-minded idiots. I'm not an egalitarian. No sir. That's what's wrong with this country, everybody thinking they're equal to everybody else, when of course they're not."

Dr. Dobbs was a real winner, I thought to myself. Was there a Mrs. Dobbs? Somehow I doubted it.

He seemed to realize he was making a bad impression. He tried something that vaguely looked like a smile. He said: "Don't mind what I say. I'm agitated, that's all. I don't normally talk politics to strangers. Anyway, this convention in Oregon.... My point was, those things are usually boring. Deadly dull. You get a thousand dentists together, what do you expect? And they're all fixated on this big hole in people's faces, you know, the oral cavity, the mouth. But there's more to people than teeth and gums and a mouth. That's where holistic dentistry comes in. I want to wake up the dental profession, if I can. OK: I also wanted to go to some of the workshops, on implants. Right now, I don't do implants. But implants are the coming thing. There's a lot of money in implants."

I had to agree. My own implant cost me a fortune. Not covered by dental insurance, either, for some mysterious reason. "So," I said. "You were at this convention. And Colegrove went too." He gave me a strange look. "Yes, Colegrove went. But not with me, like I said. And he didn't travel alone. I'm not interested in his private life, so let's not talk about that."

Which was too bad. I would have loved to know who Dr. Colegrove traveled with, and why. I assume it was a woman. And not his wife. Otherwise, why say he wasn't "alone?" But Dobbs had no intention of letting me in on the secret; instead, he went on with his story.

"Anyway, I had a long hard day. I gave my talk, it went well I thought, but it was tiring. And then I went to a whole bunch of sessions, on periodontitis, implants, other things, some interesting, some disappointing. It's always that way. So it was evening and I was bone tired. I just wanted to relax. There was going to be a big cocktail party, but I don't like that sort of thing. I had just come out of a session, 'Eight Habits of a Healthy Dental Office,' and I met this young woman. Funny, she wasn't wearing a conference badge, but I didn't make anything of it at the time. She was good looking, and like I said, I was tired and bored. She smiled at me, then she asked me, was I going to the cocktail party, and she called me Ryan, well, of course, I had a name tag on, but somehow, I felt, she was.... well, attracted to me. I said no, I hate cocktail parties. She said, so do I. I said to her, are you a dentist? She said, no, not exactly. I'm interested in dentistry, you know, as a branch of human learning, or something like that. I'm not sure what she said. I didn't care. Well, to make a long story short, she said, are you going to have dinner, and I said yes, and she said, do you have plans, and I didn't. We had dinner together, I had a few drinks, and she said, well, let's go up to my room, and I said sure. Frankly, by that time, I was thinking, she wants it as much as I do. We ordered more liquor from room service—she had this beautiful room, near the top of the hotel, great view, what they call the concierge floor. One thing led to another, and we ended up having sex."

Where was this going? Why was Ryan Dobbs telling me this? I just said something like "Uh huh," and let him go on.

"Right. We had sex. And... well, this is the embarrassing part. There we were, right in the middle of things, we were on the bed—I don't want to get too graphic, but it was hot and heavy—and somehow, she knocked over this big lamp on an end table, I'm not sure how, but anyway, down she went, with me on top of her, but the lamp crashed into her. It wasn't my fault, it was hers, I mean, maybe it wasn't anybody's fault, it just happened. Anyway, she was hurt, and she started screaming and wailing... I called the hotel operator, get a doctor, I said, there's been an accident. I put my clothes on real fast, but she was naked, I thought, she should put something on.... But she was crying, she was bleeding, her hand, and her face, her face was all cut up, I mean, she wasn't going to die or anything like that, but she was hurt; it was a mess, I don't know what else, maybe bruises, cuts on her face, her body, and she was getting hysterical. It was awful. God, nothing like this ever happened to me before."

"And you, were you hurt?"

"Not in the slightest. Just her."

"And now she's suing you, right? Is that the problem?"

"Me? No way. Some hotel doctor came, and somebody from the hotel, maybe a house detective, I don't know. She insisted on me making some sort of statement, what happened, then I got out of there as fast as I could. And then, what do you think? She calls me up, this is weeks later, and she says she's suing her company, the company she works for. You won't believe this, but she's trying to get workers' compensation. I said to her, workers' compensation? What are you talking about? You want compensation, from your company? What company's that? She said, she thinks she's entitled. She was on the job. I mean, is she nuts? On the job? Pick up a guy at a dental convention, screw him, and that's on the job? But she's serious about it. She said, this was a business trip, and the sex was part of the business. I told her, I don't get it. What kind of business? I thought, is she some kind of hooker? I didn't pay her or anything. How could she be entitled to compensation? Are hookers covered by workers' comp anyway?"

"I don't think so," I said. "But if she was actually on the job, then I suppose she could be covered. Seriously." I was trying to remember what I knew about workers' compensation. I don't usually handle such cases. "Suppose you're a traveling salesman. You check into a motel. There's a fire that night, and you're hurt. You can get workers' compensation. You're on the job 24 hours a day, that's the way the law looks at it. I mean, if traveling is part of the job. You have to go, let's say, to Denver on business; well, you've got to check into a hotel, right? So you're covered if there's a hotel fire or that sort of thing. Was she a salesman of some kind? Maybe she was at the convention to sell some sort of dental equipment."

"She was no salesman," he said. "It turns out, she works for an insurance company. It's a big company. They do dental insurance, I guess that's the connection, company's based in Sacramento, you know, here in California. She's an investigator for the insurance company. So she says she was there on business, at my hotel, doing some kind of investigation I think. And now the company is conducting a huge investigation themselves, they're resisting her claim; I think it's going to end up in court. She tells me I'm a witness. What I want to know is, do I have to cooperate? I don't want to. I don't want anything to do with it. That's why I thought, I need a lawyer. I need advice."

I guess if you need advice, and only a bottom feeder can give it to you, well, then you have to consult a bottom feeder. I said, "If there's a hearing, in some administrative agency or in court, and you're called as a witness, yes, you have to go."

"But the whole thing is ridiculous," he said, getting fairly angry and raising his voice. I don't like angry clients. They're even worse than clients who burst into tears. "What kind of a country is this? The whole legal system is crazy. This woman, this bitch, she picks up an innocent stranger, she plays him like a banjo, she goes to bed with him, and that's business? She knocks over a lamp in the middle of screwing him, and the company is supposed to pay? I can't believe it."

"Well, to be honest," I said, "she has a case. She can

claim she was doing her job...."

"Her job!" he said, raising his voice in anger. "Her job is sexual intercourse—that's her job?"

"Hold on," I said. "No, of course, that's not her job. Eating isn't her job either. But she's away on business, right? She goes to a restaurant, and she slips and falls and breaks her leg, well, she gets workers' compensation. So suppose she knocked over a lamp, and it hurt her—forget the sex part—she'd have a claim, wouldn't she? Is this so different?"

"Yes, it's different," he said, in a grim tone of voice.

"But why is it different? OK: let's try it this way. Suppose she is traveling on business, she checks into a hotel, she's with her own husband, they're having sexual intercourse, and she knocks over a lamp. Wouldn't she have a legitimate claim? She wasn't doing anything wrong, and she was on the job, sort of...."

I too was wondering, exactly what kind of a job this woman had. And what she was investigating? Was it sheer coincidence that she came on to Ryan Dobbs? Or had she identified him in advance as.... As what?

I kept these thoughts to myself. As for Ryan, there was no sign he had heard a word I said. If he had, he paid no attention. He kept grousing and complaining, showing extreme irritation. "I don't need this. Bad enough, this whole Maggie business. Damn woman had to go and get herself killed. She hated me, tell you the truth. Anyway, the police, they've been questioning me. Bunch of stupid overgrown oafs. If it was up to me, I'd privatize the whole police department. Let people arrange their own security. Couldn't be worse than what we've got now. These goons, they kept asking me, where was I that morning? At home, I told them; I told Colegrove, I wouldn't come in that day, I had things I wanted to take care of at home. Oh, what things? They kept asking. Of course they don't believe me. Why weren't you at work, and so on. I wanted to say, none of your damn business. But they'd probably pistol-whip me. They're drunk with power, I tell you. You take some idiot, you give him a badge, and a gun, and he thinks he can lord it all over you. Well, I don't like it."

I mumbled some sort of agreement.

"Maggie, Maggie: they wouldn't let go of this. Was it true that I had fierce arguments with her about politics? That's all I need... on top of that convention business, which is driving me crazy. I can't believe what's going on. The system has gone stark raving mad. It's like the McDonald's hot coffee thing, even worse. People want easy money, it's like candy. They think money grows on trees. The liberals, and believe me, this area is lousy with them, they keep going on and on about big corporations. This Maggie, she was that kind of person; I mean, if you said 'corporation' to her, it was like saying 'Hitler.' I said, who do you think made this country great? It was people who took risks, that's who. Entrepreneurs. They founded these corporations. They fought hard. Competition, that's what made this country what it is. Or what it was. The law of the jungle. Survival of the fittest. It's a law of nature. I mean, the lion lying down with the lamb? Forget it. The lion isn't going to lie down with the goddamn lamb; he's going to eat the lamb. That's what life is all about. Problem today, we just pamper people, they have 'entitlements.' I hate the word. They take away my hard-earned money, taxes, taxes, taxes. Then they hand it over to these moochers."

Did he think he was making a good impression on me? Or convincing me he was right? No; but I never argue with a client. I let his words wash over me, like gentle rain, even though they were anything but gentle.

He seemed to realize, after a bit, that he was wasting his stump speech on me—not that he had any idea about my politics, which I keep to myself; but he was aware that this right-wing talk was simply not germane. The issue was the convention, the lamp, and the woman with her compensation claim. I told him, as gently as I could, yes, once again, there very well might be a case... and if there was, if it came up, either in court or before some sort of tribunal, then, yes, he would have to testify. The whole idea seemed to infuriate him. I could tell just by looking at him. But he kept quiet this time.

Was Ryan Dobbs a suspect? Was this, maybe, a hate crime? He certainly harbored a lot of anger and hate. Maybe people like Ryan Dobbs sometimes snap, pick up their uzi, and go out and kill people. Maybe he killed Maggie because she was a liberal Democrat and she bugged him beyond his power to resist. Maybe he was a member of some fringe group, the Aryan Nation or something along those lines, and they assigned him to kill registered Democrats.

I had trouble convincing myself. He was a dentist, for God's sake. Maybe a libertarian dentist, maybe a dentist who has been drinking the Ayn Rand koolaid, but a dentist nonetheless. I wonder if there's ever been a study, how many dentists kill people. Pretty few I would imagine.

But there's a first time for everything.

12

The trouble is, if you start with the list of suspects, eliminate the dentists, eliminate the dental assistants, eliminate Chloe, eliminate Stanley, eliminate Milo Feigenblatt and his wife Zelda, then who on earth are you left with? The mysterious Mr. Borromeo, whoever he is... and the president of Xyloquex, who I hadn't yet met. And, oh yes, Maggie's abusive ex-husband, who may or may not be the same person as Mr. Borromeo.

Stanley though. Was I dismissing him too quickly? I had unfinished business with Stanley. I kept wondering, how can I get him to answer the question that was on my mind? I'm very well aware of the lawyer-client privilege, and I know that Stanley had perfectly good reasons not to tell me some of the things I wanted to know. But I decided to try him anyway. Nothing ventured, nothing gained.

I called him on the phone. "What's this about, Frank?" he asked, in a suspicious tone. Well, lawyers have a right to be suspicious.

"You know, there are things I really would want to know about, and I ask you, and you keep dodging the issue."

"Like what, for instance?"

"Like, what were you doing at the dentist's office that morning."

"What do people usually do? They go to have their teeth done."

"You didn't have an appointment," I said. "You're not

on the list of people who had appointments."

"Frank," he said, "you're bugging me. Bad enough I had to find a dead body and walk around with my fly open. Bad enough I have to talk to the police constantly, and deal with reporters, too; the local papers, they want to run a story about this. They're after me, I'm the guy who was on the scene, can we run a story on you, blah blah. To top it off, I've got Frank May, boy detective, on my case. OK: you want the truth: I went there to kill Maggie. I wanted to kill her because I'm a split personality. When the moon is full, I turn into a werewolf. I'm the only lawyer werewolf in San Mateo County."

"I think the bar is full of werewolves," I said.

"Give up, Frank," he said. "You're not going to get anywhere with me."

I sighed. "OK, Stanley, you win."

There was a long pause. "Stanley, are you still there?"

"I'm here, Frank. I was thinking, should I throw you a bone? I don't know why I should do you a favor, and you're bugging me, but you're a good man, Frank, so I'll give you a hint. You know, probate records are public. Anybody can look at them."

"Of course I know that, Stanley."

"OK. Then take a look at the will."

"The will? Whose will? Maggie's will?"

He laughed. "Maggie's will? She left everything to her daughter. No, not her will. The will of Dr. Morris Sylvester."

Then he hung up the phone.

13

This of course left me totally perplexed. What on earth did the late Dr. Sylvester have to do with all this? Why was Stanley acting so damn mysterious? And then I remembered the odd thing Maggie had said: that she knew about somebody who had killed somebody. Who could this victim be? Was it possible that somebody killed poor Dr. Sylvester? And was this why Maggie was killed: because she knew too much? It was an intriguing thought. But if so, we still had a real puzzle. Why did this somebody wait so long? I didn't remember when exactly Dr. Sylvester died, but it must have been more than a year before all this, maybe longer.

Stanley had told me to look at Dr. Sylvester's will. I had to admit I was extremely curious. So, despite a lot of things to do—things which were going to put food on the table and buy clothes for the girls—I decided to do exactly that. So I went to the county courthouse and asked to see the file for the estate of Morris Sylvester. I couldn't imagine why old Dr. Sylvester and his estate had anything to do with Maggie's death, or anything else, for that matter. But I was curious. Stanley must have had something in mind.

As it happened, I had legitimate business in the probate court. It concerned the estate of one of my clients, Sigmund Oberschuss. A lawyer I knew used a euphemism to refer to a dead client: he would say that the man's estate had finally "ripened." Well, Sigmund had been extremely ripe—he was over 90 when he finally passed on. He had been demented for years, the flame sputtered but never went out, year after year, frustrating his two greedy sons and their equally rapacious wives, who had been hovering in the wings like vultures, eager to get at the old man's money. That money was tied up in a trust they could not touch—at least as long as old Sigmund lived. Even more frustrating were the horrendous costs of Sigmund's last years—twenty-four hour nursing care eating away at the estate. They must have breathed a sigh of relief when Sigmund at long last had the decency to die.

I had papers to file for Sigmund's estate. It was thus a golden opportunity to look at the file of Dr. Sylvester. As I examined the file, I found out a number of things. First of all, the good doctor left behind quite a bit of money. I suppose if you work as a dentist, if you're a frugal bachelor, living with your aged mother Mildred, and if you never go anywhere and do anything, and also invest rather shrewdly, you can end up as a very rich corpse. Dr. Sylvester left more than $10,000,000 behind.

It was Dr. Sylvester's will that intrigued me. Stanley had drafted the will, and it was nicely professional. It was many pages long. It was also quite old—it predated the death of Mildred Sylvester. Essentially, Dr. Sylvester left his entire estate, in trust, "for so long as my beloved mother, Mildred Sylvester, may live," with a proviso allowing the trustee, Wells Fargo, to invade the trust for her benefit, if needed. And then, on her death, he left one half of the estate to various charities, and the other half to "my dear friend and colleague, Caleb Colegrove." The will named as executor Dr. Caleb Colegrove. The estate, by the way, was in apple-pie order. Dr. Sylvester must have had a good accountant. The assets were sound and straightforward, and there were no debts to speak of.

The will surprised me though: all that money left to Caleb Colegrove. At least under the original will. There was also, surprisingly, a codicil to the will, and it was somewhat shocking. A codicil is an amendment to a will. This codicil was short and written entirely in Dr. Sylvester's handwriting. That kind of will or codicil is valid in California; it's called a holograph. It's rarely a good idea to amend your will that way, but still, some people do it. The codicil itself took my breath away. It revoked the gift to Caleb Colegrove entirely. It made a few small gifts, to friends, a slightly bigger gift to a cleaning lady... and then it left half of the remaining estate to an organization called Dentists Without Borders, which "brings the benefits of modern dentistry to people in third world countries." The other half was left to the "Dahlia-Growers League of Northern California, in memory of my beloved mother, Mildred Sylvester."

That was it. As I said, a codicil is an amendment to a will; it leaves the original will intact, except for the parts that the codicil actually changes. Because the codicil said nothing about the executor, this meant that Caleb Colegrove was still in charge of the estate. My guess is that Dr. Sylvester simply forgot about the issue. But this meant that Colegrove had the duty of administering an estate, under a will which cut him out of millions and millions of dollars. That must have been annoying, to say the least.

You had to wonder: why did Dr. Sylvester write this codicil? Why did he change his mind about his "dear friend and colleague Caleb Colegrove?" And did Colegrove know about this change? Was it possible that he knew about the will, the one that left him a ton of money, but not about the codicil, in which Morris Sylvester changed his mind? If so, then he had a powerful motive for killing Dr. Sylvester. The codicil was probably drawn up in secret. You don't need witnesses for a handwritten codicil. Nor do you need to consult a lawyer; a lawyer would draw up a regular will, with witnesses and all. So very likely, Caleb knew nothing about the codicil. Of course, as soon as Dr. Sylvester died, and the codicil came to light, he obviously found out the true state of affairs. That could have been quite a shock.

I wished I could ask Stanley for more information,

but I wondered if I would get any answers. He was the lawyer for the estate, and therefore, I assume, he was the lawyer for Caleb Colegrove, the executor of Dr. Sylvester's estate. It had been a bit indiscreet of Stanley even to tell me to look at the file. I noticed, too, the date of the codicil—only a few weeks before Dr. Sylvester died. My heart was pounding. Was this a viable theory: Caleb thought he was going to get all this money; he killed poor Dr. Sylvester; Maggie knew about it somehow; and then he killed her? Good Lord, what was I thinking? My own dentist? The man who did my root canal work? Could this be true?

I had to find out how Dr. Sylvester died. He wasn't young—nearly 70. His mother had been in her 90's. I had always assumed he had a heart attack or something of the sort. That's what carries most of us off, unless we have cancer or some long, drawn-out thing. I do remember hearing that this was all rather sudden. I made a mental note to talk to Stanley about Dr. Sylvester's death.

14

As you can imagine, the case was very much on my mind. Especially on a Tuesday morning a few days later, when I personally entered the crime scene, though for a very mundane purpose. You recall that I had an appointment on the murder day, which of course I had to cancel. A few days later, I called and rescheduled. There was no dental crisis; it was just the usual visit to have my teeth X-rayed and serviced. "No murders this time, please," I said to the receptionist. This was a new person, hired to replace Maggie, and she found my comment extremely unfunny.

The new person, whose name was Tiffany, was a rather blank-looking woman, slightly overweight, in her 30's I would say. Chloe was there too, sitting next to her. I plopped down in a chair, to wait my turn, in the tiny waiting room. I've often wondered: why do they make you wait? Is it a matter of policy? Was it designed to spread the word that this dentist and his staff are terrifically busy, or what? Or was it just legitimate scheduling problems?

The selection of magazines was quite poor, but they did have old copies of National Geographic. I immersed myself in an article about the hunting of narwhals. I had only the tiniest of interests in narwhals, and I was about to move on to an article on giant fish of the Amazon basin, which seemed a bit more interesting, when the dental assistant, Charlotte, called me in.

I noticed the layout of the office, with (naturally)

more than a patient's usual interest. There was the reception room, where I had been sitting, with its tiny waiting area off to the side. The office as a whole was L-shaped, and the reception area—together with the fatal bathroom—was in the small leg of the L. Whoever was in the back, Dr. Colegrove and whoever else, would not normally be able to see what was going on in the reception area, unless they came out of their dens and actually walked into that part of the office. In the back part, the big leg of the L, there were several rooms, each of which had a dentist's chair and the other torture instruments of the trade; there was also another bathroom, and a door to the outside at the very end of the corridor. I was dying to know whether this door was locked or not—that is, whether somebody could come into the office that way. I of course always went in and out by way of the front entrance.

Charlotte Sprague, the dental assistant who usually took care of me, was a woman of 45 or 50, with dyed red hair. She was attractive—well, striking I think is the word. She was quite tall—not as tall as Zelda, but tall enough. Taller than me, for one thing, not that that matters. She was a bit thin and bony, but within reasonable limits. Charlotte had worked in the office as long as I can remember. At any rate, as long as I had been Dr. Colegrove's patient, which was about six years. Before that, my dentist was a man named Joseph Glutz, who retired and moved to Las Vegas. I personally would rather die than live in Las Vegas, but apparently it is quite popular with retired people, so they obviously seem quite content to die in Las Vegas, as well as to live there.

Charlotte had always been the one who tended to my teeth. Not that I knew her well: conversations in the dentist chair tend to be quite rudimentary, since your mouth is open much of the time. I remember hearing that Charlotte had not been in the office that fateful morning. That struck me as odd. Dobbs wasn't there, and Charlotte wasn't there either. The office was unusually empty, considering that it was an ordinary working day. As far as I knew, the only people there were Maggie, Dr. Colegrove, and the other assistant, Estelle. Was this strange situation somehow connected with the crime? You had to wonder.

I settled into the dentist's chair, leaned back, and opened my mouth dutifully. "We don't need to do X-rays today," she said. "You did them last time."

I mumbled something; I was glad, in fact, to avoid the X-ray machine. I hate the X-rays. Not the X-rays themselves, but they stick something in your mouth, some sort of X-ray film I think, and I gag on it every time.

Charlotte stared at my mouth, and her face looked grim. "You have a real build-up of plaque, did you know that?" She said it in a tone that a doctor might use in telling a patient he had Stage IV liver cancer. "I'm afraid, at the rate you're going, you're going to need a periodontist. Do you floss regularly?"

"Actually, I don't," I said. In fact, I don't floss at all. But I didn't dare confess to that cardinal dental sin.

"Really, Mr. May. Doctor recommends flossing. Or would you rather use the little plastic sticks? They're not as good as flossing, but they're better than nothing. And do you brush for a full two minutes?"

I said I did. A little white lie. I brush my teeth for a full ten seconds, if you want to know the truth.

She poked about with little picks and scrapers for a while, no doubt to attack the dreadful plaque that was causing the trouble. Then she rinsed out my mouth, and started again.

"I understand you're working on this case," she said. "I mean, what happened to Maggie. That was so terrible. I think it must have been a crazy person, don't you think? I'm so lucky I wasn't there that morning."

My mouth was wide open, with a wad of cotton stuck inside next to the cheek. I couldn't have commented even if I wanted to. When I had a chance, I emitted a grunt that was designed to sound vaguely like agreement.

She started picking with the sharp thing between my teeth again. "Estelle was here," she said. "She was the only one. I mean, the only dental assistant that morning. Of course Doctor was here. Have you met Estelle?" I shook my head no. "The patients really like Estelle. I stayed away. Do you know why I wasn't here? I think I should tell you because... because you're working on the case. I feel you should know."

I wanted to tell her that I wasn't really "working on the case," but in the first place my mouth was still open, and in the second place, I knew it would be hopeless. She obviously didn't expect any response from a man with a wide-open mouth; she was currently scraping away at my molars. "I stayed away because I was afraid. I was afraid of this mysterious person, Hendrik Borromeo, or whatever name he gives. The phantom patient I call him, but it isn't funny. I was really afraid of him."

She paused, put some sort of suction thing in my mouth to get rid of the saliva, and then looked at me, still holding some kind of sharp implement in her hand. "Or it could have been my ex-boyfriend, Wilson. He's insanely jealous. That's why I broke up with him. He was depressed most of the time. I was afraid he might get violent. You know, all that suppressed anger. I read somewhere, in a magazine, that people who are depressed are really angry. The anger just goes inside. That's what makes them depressed, but then it can burst out of them, you know? I was terrified."

I grunted to let her know I was listening.

"He was much, much younger than I am," she said. "I know, today that doesn't make any difference, but still, you have to wonder.... I met him in a bar. I know what you're thinking, Charlotte, you go to bars? I don't, I really don't. It was at this dental convention, years ago. He seemed depressed. And he was so good-looking. I went over to him, honest to God, I never did anything like that before. He worked for this company, he was a salesman, dental equipment. I had just gotten a divorce. My husband left me. He went to Arizona. Left me behind, struggling with a child. The life of a single parent, it's not easy. I... just couldn't cope. But that's not the point. I gave the child up, my boy, to people who could care for him. Do you think that was an awful thing to do?"

She paused, rinsed out my mouth again, and went right on: "Anyway, Wilson was sitting there, at the bar, and he started crying. Imagine, crying! A man like that. I found out later, he was a very emotional person. He had terrible mood swings. Well: here he was, sobbing away, this young man, and he was frankly very attractive. And I was so lonely. I went over and said, do you want to talk about it? I said, I felt like crying myself. Anyway, it turned out, he did want to talk. And he had broken up with somebody. Just like me. He had been living with a woman twenty-five years older than he was. Was he looking for a mother, you have to ask? Anyway, we had this in common—we were failures in the love department. I thought, maybe it's fate that brought us together. We started talking and, well, one thing led to another."

I nodded.

"It was great at first. He tried hard. But I felt... deep down, it wasn't right. The age difference.... And his depression. After I read all this material on depression, I realized it had to be suppressed rage, just had to be, although I have to admit, he never showed any signs of violence. Mind you, he never laid a finger on me, but I could see the suppressed anger, that's the phrase this psychiatrist used, Wilson went to him, and we had couples therapy.... I'm rambling, I'm sorry, and your gums are bleeding a bit, let me take care of that."

"Gums?"

"We have to be, oh, so careful with gums," she said. "Gums are the weak point, for many people. I'll give you a pamphlet about gums. But where was I: oh, Wilson, he just couldn't shake the depression; he would sit there, how should I say it, brooding, if you know what I mean. He would sit for hours, just staring into space. I would say, Wilson, what's on your mind, tell mommy—he used to call me mommy—but he would just shake his head. Finally I couldn't take it anymore. I told him, this isn't working out. Actually, I had found somebody else. I didn't mention that to Wilson. I didn't want to hurt him. But I had discovered what love really is, what it means. Wilson, I said, my darling, you're young, you have your whole life ahead of you. And he sobbed and sobbed, but he did go away. Still, he's been hanging around here—did you know that? Of course you didn't. How could you. This mystery patient, I thought, maybe it's Wilson, maybe he's trying to... confront me. Oh, not violently. But.... Anyway, it's because of that, because of Wilson, that's why I stayed away. I thought he could be this Borromeo person. He knows I won't answer his phone calls or emails, so... he thought he'd try me here."

She was polishing my aching teeth with some sort of polish that smelled like wintergreen, and then she rinsed out my mouth again. After I spit out the water I said, "You think this man was your ex-boyfriend? Some people thought it might be Maggie's ex-husband. Did she say anything much about him?"

"Oh, Maggie's ex: yes, that's possible... I know that. But it could be Wilson. He actually came over one night. He seemed so... despondent. I was afraid of him, oh, it sounds ridiculous, I was afraid he'd kill himself, not me. I told him, as gently as I could, I never wanted to see him again, please, I said, this is finished. And I finally told him, I had somebody else, and he burst into tears, it was heart-breaking. I said, Wilson, control yourself. I thought I'd never get rid of him that night."

"And you think that... he was this mystery person? And he did this thing with Maggie?"

"I don't know what to think."

"But you said, he wasn't violent. Sad, depressed, but... harmless, no?"

"Yes, that's what I thought. But you never can tell, can you? Maybe something snapped. Maybe he came and he was looking for me, and maybe Maggie said something or told him he had to go, and it's like his head exploded, and... that was it...."

It really seemed unlikely to me, but I didn't say so. Instead I asked, "Did you tell this to the police?"

"Oh, yes... but whether they're going to follow up, I have no idea. I couldn't tell them where Wilson was living these days, or what he was doing. I don't have a clue. Going to school, maybe. He was at a community college, but I forget which one."

"You don't really think it's him, do you?"

She was silent for a second. "Actually, I don't. But I can't be 100% sure, can I? I just wanted to explain to you, why I wasn't here that day. Somebody did this; and I... wanted to help...."

She eased me out of the chair and took off the bib-like thing around my neck. "Let's try to do more flossing," she said. She gave me a tiny tube of toothpaste, a pink toothbrush, some floss, and a box of the little sticks that I (sometimes) use to clean my teeth. "Wait here a moment," she said. She disappeared, then came back and said: "Doctor said he wants to see you."

"The doctor? What about?"

"About this cavity...."

"What cavity?" I said. "You didn't take X-rays. You didn't mention anything.... Did you see something in my mouth that looked like a cavity?"

"I'm not a dentist, Mr. May," she said. "Please wait here. Doctor will speak to you."

She left. I felt I needed to talk to her again. This ex-boyfriend idea didn't strike me as plausible, but then again, it might be worth looking into. Not by me, of course, but it might be something I could report to Maggie's daughter, or to Zelda. Actually, Maggie's ex-husband sounded more likely.

After a short wait, Dr. Colegrove came into the room, all professional-looking, in his white coat and his most dentist-like manner. In a very professional style, he told me my situation was good, no cavities. He repeated the advice about flossing.

"Charlotte said I had a cavity."

"Well, actually, you don't," he said. "I told her to say that. I didn't want you to run away before I saw you. Look, Frank, I've got to talk to you. Do you have some time today?"

"Three o'clock?"

"No, that won't work. I've got a patient then, Mrs. Gellers, do you know her?" I didn't. "Lovely woman. It's a root canal problem. I can't cancel her. But... can we have our little chat later? Say six o'clock, in your office?"

I had been hoping to go home early and relax. But I said "sure."

I wondered what he had in mind. There was no point guessing.

As I went out, Charlotte came after me and reminded me about my duties: "I'd like you to floss, Frank. Really. I gave you some floss. Use it, Frank. Believe me, it'll do wonders for your mouth."

I took the floss. I could always throw it away, or give it to Celia. Celia flosses regularly. Rain or shine.

15

It was a long, boring afternoon; I worked on a memo and had an interminable talk with one of my most obnoxious clients. My main function with this man, who owned an orthopedic shoe store, was to talk him out of suing other people. I usually succeeded, when he realized how much it would cost him to get his revenge on the couple who lived in the condo just above him. It seemed they kept their windows open, played loud music at night, "stuff I can't stand," as he put it. "And I swear they're drunk half the time."

"But what's the point, Jonathan?" I said to him. "Do you really need this extra aggravation?"

Dr. Colegrove appeared promptly at six. He looked extremely troubled. "Frank, I have to talk to you. It's important. I just have to talk to somebody. I've got to get things off my chest. There are things... well, let's say I haven't been leveling with you. Not really."

"What do you mean?"

"I haven't given you the whole story."

I said, "That's OK, Caleb. Look: I know I've been your lawyer in the past, but, well, if it's about anything right now, remember, you don't have any obligation to me— you don't have to tell me anything, unless you want to."

"I know that, Frank. I've got a lawyer. Stanley. But... I think you're somebody a man could confide in."

"Thanks, Caleb," I said. I couldn't help wondering. Why didn't he want to talk to Stanley? Stanley had been at the dentist's office that morning. He had no actual appointment. Had he gone there to see Caleb for some other reason? But if so, wouldn't Caleb rather confide in him?

Caleb sat across from me. He was sweating, I noticed. He was clearly agitated. "Look," he said. "This awful business, with Maggie, maybe there's more to it than... meets the eye. Something's going on. I'm not sure I know what it is. Like, this mysterious person, Hendrik Borromeo, this guy who made an appointment, then never showed up. As far as we know, that is. I think I know who he is. And I don't think he had anything to do with Maggie. I really don't."

Of course I was curious. "You know who he is?"

"Well, I think I do. I think he's an investigator, or whatever you call these people. I think it has something to do with a lawsuit against me. Or maybe it's something worse...."

"You're talking in riddles, Caleb. I don't know what you're getting at."

"There's a malpractice case against me. This family, the Getz family, they're suing me. I had this patient, Monty Getz. There was this terrible incident. The anesthesia... well, it went bad. This man, this patient, he started having this awful reaction.... It's hard for me to talk about it. He suffered some kind of cardiac arrest. We called 911.... I was going to take out one of his wisdom teeth. Completely routine, Frank, honest. He was 56 years old. Overweight. Big paunch, you know what I mean. Maybe he had a history, I just don't know. Oh, God, I remember it so vividly. I was in the midst of the extraction, and he made this ghastly noise and slumped down. They rushed him to the hospital. He lingered a while, then they pulled the plug. I was so traumatized, I couldn't practice for two months. I took a kind of sabbatical, Dr. Sylvester, he took over my practice. Then when his mother died, he was in worse shape than I was, and I came back and started functioning again. Anyway, this man, he had a son, Monty Jr., who filed a lawsuit against me.... That's bad enough. But there's so much bitterness there. He thinks I killed his father. There was an investigation, cleared me completely, of course; after all, it was just one of these things. But the family, they just wouldn't buy it. They blame me. This Monty Jr., he's suing me for millions of dollars."

"And you think this Hendrik person...."

"This lawsuit, it's going to drive me crazy. They've got lawyers, I've got lawyers. Not you, Frank, I know you don't do this sort of thing, you need a specialist, well, you're aware of that. And not just Stanley. I mean, lawyers who defend this kind of lawsuit. It's costing me a fortune, and I really can't afford it right now. At first I thought, this guy, this Hendrik, maybe he's some sort of investigator. But then I had this terrible thought. I think maybe it's the son, Monty Jr. He's a real lunatic. He came by once, bold as brass, burst into the office—he was fat just like his father, big beer belly and a red face, disgusting man—and he said, you killed my father, we're going to get you. Said it over and over again, you killed my father. I threatened to call the police."

"And?"

"Well, he left, but screaming and ranting. I think he's absolutely insane. I couldn't work the rest of the afternoon. Mitzi Warren was here, my patient, she was sitting in the dentist chair, and I was filling a cavity, in her molar. It was such a painful scene. I told Mitzi, look, can you come back, this was just too upsetting. I mean, I have feelings. I was angry, frightened, upset. She left. She never came back, by the way. I lost a patient because of that guy. She went right over to Flansbaum. OK, one patient, I can live with that. But I can imagine the gossip, she's a woman with a poisonous tongue. And I dread the lawsuit, going to court, the publicity...."

"I know how you feel, Caleb. It must have been a terrible thing for you."

"Absolutely terrible. Frank, you're not mad at me, are you? Because I went to Roth and Brombeck? I didn't come to you. Or Stanley. I know you two don't do this kind of work...."

"Please, Caleb. It's OK. No problem. I would have just referred you to them, or somebody like them. You did the right thing."

"I knew you'd understand. Frank, I'm in deep trouble."

"Trouble? You mean the lawsuit."

"Yes, that. Of course. I swear, I didn't do anything wrong. But the other side, they hired these quack doctors, quack lawyers, quack dentists, they have people who are going to make ridiculous statements, things about the anesthetic—believe me, Frank, there's nothing to it, but they can make something out of nothing. These lawyers... I'm sorry, I don't mean you. You're a good man, Frank, but those others.... This could cost me my license. You know those insurance companies, they're rapacious, too. And then the family, this son and his wife, they have these fancy lawyers, they want to cut off my balls, it's going to cost me a fortune either way. I have insurance, but they want so much more.... And Maggie...."

"Maggie? What about Maggie?"

"She was there the day it happened.... I mean, the day the patient died. I told her, Maggie, call 911, when I saw the man slumped in the chair, I was standing there, for a second I was paralyzed. Maggie, I said, get an ambulance. So she made the call. Now they claim that she was a witness. She was there... I mean, not in the room, but she was in the office, it was late, late in the afternoon, it was actually after hours. The man was an emergency he said, because of a toothache, so I said, sure come in, and I asked Maggie to stay, Maggie and the assistant too...."

"Which one?"

"Charlotte."

"And... won't they back you up? I mean, Maggie's dead, so I guess she can't... but Charlotte, she's a witness too, isn't she?"

"I mean, Maggie being dead, that's a problem for me. I was counting on her. She would have told them good things, I mean things in my favor; she'd tell them everything was done the way it was supposed to. And Charlotte, well, yes, she can testify too, and she's actually more important, in a way, because after all she's a dental technician—Maggie was just a receptionist. But I don't think she'd make a good witness, Charlotte. I don't think that would work out. No, not at all."

"Why is that, Caleb?"

He was quiet for a while. I was beginning to get an idea, but I didn't dare say it out loud. "She just wouldn't be a good witness. And she wouldn't want to get involved."

I said nothing. I think I knew. From little hints, and things I had seen in the office.

"And there's something else," he said. "I need your help. I want... can I get a restraining order?"

"A restraining order?"

"Yes. I know about these things. I talked to Maggie. She was afraid of her ex-husband. Did you know that? It's funny. This mystery guy, Hendrik Borromeo, all of us think we know who that is, and we're worried. Maggie and her ex-husband. She said, if he was around, she'd get a restraining order. But she never did anything about it. I'd like to know, Frank, how you go about getting that kind of thing."

"Against him? Against Maggie's ex-husband? What has that got to do with you, Caleb?"

"Nothing... that isn't the person I'm worried about. I'm worried about Wilson Getz."

"Wilson Getz? Who's that? Wasn't Getz the name of the family, the man who died in your office?"

"Yes, yes. But Wilson isn't part of the lawsuit. It's about him and Charlotte."

"I had a conversation with her, myself," I said. He looked surprised. I went on: "She told me something about that," I said. "This is a young man? Somebody she had been with for a while?"

"Yes. Wilson Getz is Monty's nephew. Or cousin, I'm not sure. The whole family, they used to be patients of mine. Of course, since the accident.... And maybe that had something to do with the breakup, between Charlotte and Wilson. Anyway, she wants to get rid of him. He's not a bad person, but he's obsessed with her. He's following her around, maybe you could even call it stalking. I told her, Charlotte, really, there must be a way to get rid of him once and for all. That's when I thought about a restraining order."

"But is she actually afraid of him? I got the impression he was harmless."

"Is it harmless to be followed around, night and day? Anyway, I think the whole family is crazy. I'm thinking of Charlotte's welfare. She's been with me for years, and... it's not easy to get good dental assistants these days. Maybe Wilson is our mystery patient. I haven't talked to her about this restraining order, it's just something that popped into my mind. Of course, it'll cost money, I suppose, and she doesn't have much money; that's why I'd like to help her out."

We talked for a while about restraining orders. I really doubted that this was an appropriate situation. And, to be honest, I didn't think Caleb was giving me the whole story. I had my own suspicions. And they turned out to be right, as I found out the very next day.

We'll come to that. What I couldn't get out of my mind was something else: Maggie. She told Stanley that she knew about somebody killing somebody. Could she have meant Caleb Colegrove? I had been thinking that maybe she was referring to the death of Morris Sylvester... and that was still possible. Did she mean Caleb? The story would also fit Caleb in another way: the dead patient. Was there more to the death of Monty Getz than Caleb let on? The death itself was hardly a secret.... Unless there was something about it that Caleb wasn't telling me. Unless he deliberately killed the man who was sitting in the dentist's chair.... But if so, why?

And... the absurd story, about Maggie and blackmail. Could that possibly be true?

16

I found one of my suspicions confirmed, the very next day. I was on my lunch hour. It was a beautiful day, balmy, sunny, bright. A typical day in California. No wonder there are millions of us in this state, and very few in Alaska. Anyway, I decided it was just the day for sushi. I went to one of my favorite places, Bengoshi's. The place was crowded, but I sat at the counter, reading a book and savoring the meal. I love sushi. It's the sheer madness of it. Raw fish and seaweed. Chopsticks, wasabi, ginger. It's soul food, as far as I'm concerned. As the kids would say, sushi is cool! And it's basically healthy too. I do draw the line at some things which the Japanese no doubt love— sea urchin for one. Or raw shrimp. Or octopus. It tastes like leather. Not that I ever tasted leather.

I enjoyed the meal thoroughly, paid the bill, and left the restaurant. I was surprised to see Charlotte, standing just at the side of the entrance. I said hello, but was surprised when she said, "I saw you in there, Frank, and it looked like you were finishing up—you were paying the bill. Do you have a minute or two?"

"Sure, Charlotte. What's up?"

"I need to talk to you, is this a good time?"

"It is, actually. But... don't you have to get back to work?"

"It's OK," she said. "Estelle is handling things. Can I come with you to your office?"

"Sure. No problem."

When we were there, I motioned her into a chair and took my place at my desk. "OK, Charlotte," I said, "what's this all about?"

She said: "Maggie's estate. I think you know that there's a lawyer, his name is Jerry Walden, and he's claiming some money from the estate, money that Maggie had in a bank account."

I was astonished. How did Charlotte know about the money?

"It wasn't really her money," Charlotte said.

"I heard about that," I said. "But, Charlotte, I have to tell you, I'm not the lawyer for Maggie's estate. That's Stanley—you know Stanley, he was a patient of Dr. Colegrove. He's handling the estate. I have nothing to do with it."

She seemed to hesitate. Then she said, "I know that, Frank. The problem is... and maybe you can help me, give me some advice.... The problem is, it's my money. It wasn't Maggie's. It was mine."

"Yours? But why.... Why did Maggie have it then?"

"It's money I won in Las Vegas, gambling," she said. "I won a lot of money. Most people lose money in Las Vegas, but I got lucky. I went on a trip, bus trip, with a bunch of people. I don't gamble much, ordinarily. This time, well, I guess my lucky star was shining that night. They paid me in cash. But when I got back, I didn't want people to know about this money, I didn't want people pestering me... so I gave it to Maggie, I said, keep this for me, put it in a bank account, and I'll draw it out little by little. And she agreed. I couldn't know that she'd be killed."

"OK, Charlotte," I said. "But why tell me? You hired Jerry Walden, didn't you? He's the one who spoke to Stanley; I think you must know that."

She nodded her head. "Jerry's not my lawyer anymore. He got too busy, he was just overwhelmed with work, said he couldn't handle this for the next six months.

So... we more or less decided I should go elsewhere. That's why I'm talking to you, Frank. I'd like you to be my lawyer, help me get this money back."

I said to her: "Charlotte, I love getting clients. I need clients. They pay the rent. They put food on my table. But I can't work with them unless they're honest with me. Would you be insulted if I said, I don't believe a word you said? I certainly don't believe that story about your lawyer. I mean, lawyers can be very busy; but somehow, what you said, it just doesn't ring true. And I'm a bit skeptical about the Las Vegas story. I just don't buy it. Maybe I have a suspicious mind. Do you have any kind of proof? I don't gamble, I don't go to Las Vegas, so I don't know what happens if you win money, if there's some document or whatever."

Her face looked grim. "You don't believe me?"

"Charlotte, I don't. I honestly don't."

"All right," she said. "I wasn't telling the whole truth. About Jerry Walden, for one thing. It wasn't that he got too busy. It was me. I decided I didn't want him anymore. I just didn't like him. He asked too many questions."

"Charlotte, I'll bet he didn't ask any questions I wouldn't ask myself. You're not telling me the real story. We can't go and claim that this money, this $25,000, on your say-so. It's a big part of a small estate, in fact, it's just about the biggest thing in the estate. We can't just claim it without some sort of proof. I'll bet Jerry Walden told you that. I can't tell you anything different."

She burst into tears. I reached over and handed her a tissue. I hate it when clients cry. And why was she crying? Over the $25,000? Or over the fact that none of us are likely to believe what she was telling us? Did I think she won the money in Las Vegas? Not for a minute. I suppose she told Walden that story, and he started asking, when did you go, what casino was it, and so on... and the whole story fell apart. And the reason for giving it to Maggie: that also didn't ring true. I know Jerry Walden, at least by reputation. I couldn't believe he would discard a client like a used Kleenex if he could possibly help it. She got rid of him, because she wasn't getting any traction on her claim. Maybe he was just as glad. He smelled something phony; besides, the money wasn't big enough to justify a lot of work and the whole thing would be nothing but trouble. Now she was starting all over again.

And yet: was it actually her money? Where did the money come from? I can't imagine she just dreamt the story up, or that she was inventing a big lie to squeeze money out of poor Maggie's estate. I explained to her, once again, slowly, carefully, and politely, that there was not a prayer of prying the money loose, without some sort of documentary evidence, something in writing, some proof that the money was hers—that Maggie was holding it on her behalf, in some sort of informal trust-like arrangement, or whatever.

"Do you have any document—anything at all?"

She sighed, and the tears began again. "I just trusted her.... It was just her word. Maggie was an honest woman."

I didn't doubt it. But now she was dead. I'm afraid I was not much help to Charlotte. Perhaps if she had been willing to tell me the honest truth—if she told me what was really involved. But that was too much to ask. Nothing was resolved, and she left the office still in tears.

17

I worked until six or so, and then decided enough was enough. Celia called me and asked me whether I could stop by the grocery and pick up some olive oil. "We're all out of it, and did you remember, we're having Adam Finkel for dinner again, he's coming at 7:30. I'm going to have Chloe, too. I need the olive oil desperately."

"Didn't we just have him over, honey?"

"We did. But this time, I invited Chloe, too."

I had in fact totally forgotten about the invitation. Adam Finkel, the math teacher, was one of Celia's projects. Adam was a bachelor, a very quiet guy, with a slight speech defect and some sort of skin condition, all over his face, awful-looking bumps and boils, which made him very unattractive to women, I'm sure. And to men, too, for that matter. It was Celia's ambition to get him married, or at least get him some sort of sex life. I had my doubts. There was no way Chloe would go for him.

I had the olive oil and Adam Finkel's skin on my mind, so I hardly noticed someone following me to the office parking lot. As I was opening my car door, I felt a hand on my arm, and I turned to see a youngish man, with wild spiky hair standing up from his head, hair which seemed bleached some variant of blond, at least in part.

I was startled to say the least. I pushed his hand away. The man said: "Please: I've got to talk to you.... I saw you before... at lunch. You were talking to Charlotte.

She went into the building with you...."

He sounded distraught. But not threatening or dangerous. And it was, after all, broad daylight. My first reaction had been fright. When I looked at him now, I saw there were tears in his eyes. I had the feeling I was talking to Wilson Getz. "Are you Wilson Getz?" I asked.

He nodded. "Yes... I am. And you are... who?"

"Well, I'm Frank May. I'm a lawyer."

"And you and Charlotte... you're friends.... Or maybe you're her lawyer?"

"Well, acquaintances," I said. "No, I'm not her lawyer. I mean, I'm a patient of Dr. Colegrove, and I see her when I'm there, but... aside from that, no, we hardly know each other."

"I don't believe you," he said, "people don't have these long conversations, just because they go to a dentist...."

"Really, Wilson," I said, "we were just talking. It isn't really any of your business."

"Oh, but it is.... You can't imagine how much.... I have to know," he said. "What you were talking about. I can't go on like this."

"You can't go on like what? Listen, Wilson, I'm in a hurry. I've got to get home. Could you please let go? If you've got a problem, it's no concern of mine."

He dropped his hand and stared down at the ground. He was crying bitter tears. I thought: not another one of those.

Then he said, in a kind of sobbing voice: "I love her. Charlotte. I love her madly. I want her back. Did she talk to you about me? Did you know, she's sleeping with that man, her boss, the dentist? I would have done anything for her, she was my whole life, I was willing to do anything she wanted... and then she throws me over for a dentist."

"She's sleeping with Dr. Colegrove? That's impossible."

"Impossible? Oh God, if only! No, it's true. She told me. I can't stand it. They wait until all the patients are gone, and they have sex right there in the office. Or maybe at his house, I don't know. But it's true," he said, sobbing. "That other woman, she told me."

"What other woman?"

'Her name was Margie, or something. She worked there, a receptionist."

"You mean Maggie? The one that's dead?"

He seemed genuinely surprised. "She's dead? How did she die?"

"Where have you been? It's been all over the neighborhood. She was killed by somebody. Right in the dentist's office."

He stood there open-mouthed. "Oh, my God, he killed her. He had to shut her up.... The man is a maniac."

"Who are you talking about?"

"That dentist. He's an evil man. "

"No, listen, Wilson. He didn't kill her. Anyway, I don't think he did."

But he wasn't even listening. "He's awful, awful, awful. He stole her from me. Oh, Charlotte, Charlotte, be careful, he's a dangerous man...."

He seemed so pitiful. I'm not sure what it means to wring your hands, but whatever it means, he was doing it. "Oh, Charlotte. It's killing me.... To think of her with that madman... together in Oregon...."

"Oregon?"

"Portland, that's in Oregon, isn't it? They went off together, it was some sort of convention for dentists, the two of them went, together. It was going to be a kind of honeymoon. Oh God. And he's a married man, not that he cares about that. He'd stoop to anything. I talked to Maggie, I told her everything, and she knew what was going on. She was trying to be sympathetic, help me out, the poor woman, and now you say she's dead. He must have killed her. To shut her up. Oh God. I don't know what to do."

"Wilson," I said, "you've got to get a grip on yourself. I know you're disappointed, everybody gets hurt and disappointed when there's a breakup, I know it's tough, especially if it's, well, one-sided—I mean, when the breakup's one-sided. But you're a young man, you've got your whole life ahead of you. You'll get over this, really."

I know how empty this sounded. The man seemed genuinely distraught. I kept thinking of the olive oil. Celia would be furious if I came late. Wilson clutched my arm again, as if he was clinging to me for dear life. "I'll never get over it," he said. "I'll die of a broken heart."

People don't die of broken hearts, except in Victorian novels; but I felt it was not my place to make this point. "Wilson," I said, "I'm late for something important, I really can't talk to you right now. Maybe you should talk to somebody, I mean, somebody in your church or something, a doctor maybe...." Now he was blubbering, and still holding on tightly to my arm.

"I wish I knew why she left me for that guy.... I think, Charlotte, you wouldn't do it for the money, you wouldn't sell me for $25,000...."

This really caught my attention. "$25,000? What $25,000?"

"He gave her this money.... It was all hush-hush, I said, Charlotte what is this all about? We were still together. She didn't know I knew about the money, but I found out, don't ask me how I found out, but I did. She told me some story, I didn't believe it. And then she said, well, it isn't really my money, I'm just holding on to it. So I said, what does that mean? And she said, Wilson, it's none of your business. I think she was already fooling around with him. And then she said to me... oh God, she said, Wilson, it's all over."

A torrent of words. All the while, I was trying to extricate myself. It wasn't easy. He was clutching my arm pretty tightly. I reached over and gently moved his arm away. I kept thinking of the olive oil.

"I had to see her," he said. "We weren't living together. I wanted her to move in with me, I said, what's the point of separate apartments? I had a nice little place, but she said no, she wanted her independence. I said, oh, darling, I'll give you whatever independence you want. Anything. I said, Charlotte, no strings attached. Then one day, we went to this Italian restaurant. She said, I'm on my lunch hour, but I want to talk to you. She said, Wilson, you're not going to like this. I didn't know what she was talking about. I thought she meant the pasta. It was pretty salty, and I thought that's what she meant. I said, it's OK, I don't mind salt. She said, salt, Wilson? No, I'm talking about us. It's all over. I don't even remember the rest of the meal, I was crying, making a scene, and she said, she had to go, she had patients, and I was in shock. I said, Charlotte, I love you, you can't do this. Then she was gone, and I was stumbling toward the door, and this man came and said, you didn't pay the bill.... And there I was, crying, and fumbling for my credit card, they must have thought I was crazy. And yes, I was crazy, crazy in love; you understand this, don't you, Mr. May?"

I understood only too well. And I understood, too, that Celia was waiting for her olive oil. I told him how sorry I was, but there was nothing I could do, and how about counseling? He stood there blubbering, and I felt sorry for him. But I hardened my heart and drove away.

18

Wilson had cost me some valuable time. Traffic, too, was awful—some sort of road construction held me up even more. And then, to top it off, there was a long line at the supermarket. And as luck would have it, I was standing behind a grizzled old man, who caused even further delay, even though I was in the express line. This guy proceeded to argue for what seemed hours to me, harassing the poor check-out clerk, and insisting that the store had to honor the man's coupons, clipped from a newspaper, coupons that promised two cans of Chicken of the Sea tuna fish for the price of one. "That expired last Tuesday," the clerk kept telling him, but the man kept on arguing and wrangling, until the manager finally came and either got rid of him or gave him the tuna fish... and I was finally able to buy my olive oil and go home.

When I got to the house, Celia was of course quite annoyed. She said, "Frank, I can't rely on you for anything. I really can't. And this is the wrong kind of olive oil, this is olive oil with garlic, it's California olive oil, and I distinctly told you get Italian. I don't want olive oil with garlic. I'm making swordfish, Adam doesn't eat red meat, and he's lactose intolerant, I don't use butter. I'm going to have to use Canola oil, and I don't like it. I was going to cook before he got here, but he'll be here in five minutes. Really, Frank."

The evening went badly. The fish was not a success, maybe because of the oil fiasco. Adam hardly opened his mouth. His skin disorder looked worse than ever, and he was plainly embarrassed in front of Chloe. Chloe didn't talk very much either; she was polite, but it was as plain as the nose on her face that Adam didn't interest her at all. When we finished the main course, Chloe helped me carry the plates back into the kitchen, and she said to me, "That poor man. He looks so awful. I feel sorry for him. Oh God, Frank, you and Celia weren't trying to fix me up with him, were you?"

Fortunately, at that moment I dropped a plate, which broke into a thousand pieces... and in the fuss of trying to pick up the broken crockery and vacuum the kitchen so that nobody stepped on a fragment, I didn't have to answer Chloe's question. But I assume she knew the answer already. Still, you have to try. I know my Celia. She won't give up that easily.

19

Yes, the smart thing for me to do was... nothing. Forget the whole affair. But that was psychologically impossible. I felt I had to talk to Caleb Colegrove. If Maggie really said she knew about a killing, she must have been referring to Caleb. Who else? And the victim was either Monty Getz or Morris Sylvester.

Of course, I couldn't ask him directly: did you kill so-and-so? But maybe, if I spoke to him, and asked him about a number of things, some light might be shed on this murky affair. I had learned something from poor love-lorn Wilson Getz. Caleb Colegrove was carrying on with Charlotte, his dental assistant. And somehow, this mysterious $25,000 was tied up with... well, I'm not sure what it was tied up with. Maggie's death?

So I made up my mind to have a serious talk with Caleb. At least I felt I should. Celia felt otherwise. After we did the dishes, and Chloe and Adam had gone home, we sat in the living room for a bit. It's usual to have this kind of post-mortem after a dinner party. "I'm absolutely exhausted," she said. "And it was a dreadful evening, wasn't it? In every way. The broccoli was overcooked, and the fish was undercooked. Frank, I blame you. If you hadn't been late, and then you waltz in with absolutely the wrong kind of olive oil. And Adam. He's so sweet, but he's hopeless. Still, I'm not giving up."

She was not in a great mood, but I felt I had to tell her about my own day, and particularly my little chat with

Wilson Getz. After all, this was the root cause of my late arrival and the olive oil fiasco. I felt it helped my cause. Celia had her own opinion. She said: "Frank; do me a favor. Just drop this whole business. I don't know what gets into you. You're totally incorrigible! We have a police force, don't we? They take care of these things. You absolutely must not meddle in."

"I wasn't meddling in," I said. "This Wilson guy: he grabbed me and wouldn't let go, and then he was sobbing like a baby. I couldn't just shake him off and ignore him."

Celia then proceeded to give me some excellent advice. I listened carefully, and nodded my head.

There's no point telling you about the advice. In the first place, you know what it was. And in the second place, I didn't take it. I called Caleb the next morning, and told him I needed to see him.

"What about, Frank?"

I said I didn't want to talk on the phone, and was he free for lunch? It turned out he was. "Can we get a salad somewhere?" he said. "I'm trying to lose weight."

Everybody is trying to lose weight, myself included. I mean, sporadically trying. We agreed to meet at an Italian restaurant, where there were plenty of salads, along with pizza, pasta, and other more substantial soul food.

As I left the building, I saw Judd at the corner, smoking a cigarette and staring into space. I recognized him immediately, although his hair was a different weird color from the last time and it stuck up in little spikes. I said, "Hello, Judd... how are you doing?" He gave me a suspicious stare, and answered with some sort of grunt.

"Say, Judd," I said, "I want to ask you a question."

"Yeah, what?"

"You work for this Xyloquex company, right? Did you ever see the dental assistant, Charlotte, go in and out of there?" He shook his head, no. I went on: "Did you see Maggie, the lady that got killed? Or Estelle?"

"Estelle? Who's Estelle?"

"She's the other dental assistant." This drew a blank. I said: "OK, forget her. What about the other ones?"

"Hey, man, what's it to you?"

"Oh, I'm just curious," I said, trying to sound nonchalant. "Especially about that poor woman, Maggie. The dead woman."

He shrugged his shoulders, threw the cigarette butt down on the sidewalk and crushed it with the toe of his running shoe. "Hey, maybe she did. Maybe she didn't. I don't check who goes in and who goes out, you know what I mean? Maggie. Maybe. Dunno about anybody else."

"You sure you didn't see Charlotte?"

"I told you already I didn't. Doesn't mean she wasn't there, you know? But I never seen her." Then he said, "I gotta get back," and left me standing there.

Should I believe him? People are supposed to tell lawyers the truth. If they're clients, that is. I have the feeling sometimes that everybody lies to me, including my clients. It's disheartening.

I met Caleb at the door of the restaurant, Fandango's. We found a nice, quiet booth, studied the menu, and after we placed our order, I got right to the point: "Caleb, yesterday, as I told you, I met this guy, Wilson Getz. You remember?"

"Of course I do. Wilson Getz. Part of that damn family. The ones that are suing me."

"Yes... but that's not the point I want to make, Caleb, the fact that his family is suing you. I want to bring up something else. I don't think you were quite honest with me. He said he used to be, well, involved with your assistant, Charlotte. Seemed odd—he's a lot younger than she is, but I suppose that's almost normal nowadays. Nobody's shocked by that."

"What are you driving at, Frank? He's harassing her; I asked you about a restraining order."

"Yes, but you didn't tell me the whole story, Caleb. You didn't tell me about you and Charlotte."

"What? Me and Charlotte? Well, what of it. I can't see that this is any business of yours, Frank. Really."

"I told you, he saw me talking to Charlotte, and later on, he more or less grabbed me, and poured his heart out. He said he loved her, and so on, and he said you stole her away from him."

"Again, why is this any of your business?"

"OK, in a way, it isn't... but I guess I'm your lawyer, and, uh, well I'm entitled to know the full story...."

"The full story of what, Frank? Do I have to tell you about my sex life? I think I know something about what you get when you hire a lawyer: you get legal advice, you get help on legal problems, things you ask your lawyer about; but you don't get a lot of nosy questions, on irrelevant subjects. I don't want to sound harsh, Frank, but I do resent this line of attack."

"Indulge me, Caleb," I said. "Maggie's daughter, she wants me to try to get to the bottom of this business...."

"The bottom of this business? The Maggie business? And that entitles you to find out about my personal life? That's the bottom, all right. It's bottom feeding... or call it whatever you want. Is that what this lunch is all about, Frank?"

I could see how annoyed his was, and I can't say that I blamed him. "Caleb," I said, "I apologize if I'm offending you. But this Wilson guy, he was sobbing and weeping, and he said you stole her away from him... that you and Charlotte were, well, whatever you call it these days. Boyfriend and girlfriend, partners, anyway, you know what I mean. Is this true, Caleb? You can say, no comment, or none of your business; that's OK, Caleb, but I really do have a reason for asking, it's not an irrelevant question, whatever you might think."

"It's not irrelevant? And pray tell me, why not?"

"Well... it's a matter of money. Money in the estate. Some $25,000. And it seems as if it doesn't really belong to the estate. I mean, Maggie's estate. Charlotte claims it's hers, but she tells some sort of cock-and-bull story about where it came from. Las Vegas she said. I don't really believe this story. You know what I think? I think it's your money. And what I want to know is, is this money significant? Does it have something to do with Maggie's death?"

He was extremely quiet for a bit. I wondered: had I gone too far? "Maybe it had nothing to do with anything," I said feebly.

Caleb sighed and said nothing. The waiter arrived just then with the main course. I had ravioli, Caleb had some other kind of pasta. He poked at it, with his fork, took a bite or two, then put down the fork. He looked dreadfully unhappy. I said: "You don't have to tell me anything, Caleb. I don't want to hurt your feelings, or pry into your private life. I mean, is this something painful? A painful subject?"

He said, "A painful subject? Yes, it is. Sometimes I feel like I'm living in a soap opera. This Wilson person... well, what he says, about me and Charlotte, it's actually true. I know, I'm a married man, but so what? I know you're not going to preach to me. My marriage stinks, to be perfectly honest. We're just not getting along. I mean, sometimes I feel like a rat, I blame myself, but... really, it's no marriage anymore. But, Sandra and I... there's just no chemistry there, if you know what I mean. That sounds cheap and banal. I mean, it's not a good situation, for either of us. Not anymore. Maybe I have no vocation for relationships, Frank. You know I was married before. And this time, well, we started out like a house on fire. Never mind. It's dead and gone now. For both of us."

"It happens," I said, feebly.

He went right on: "Then... along came Charlotte. Well, that's misleading. She was there all the time. I'm around her all day, I've gotten to know her, and she's, well, she's such a positive person, strong, a strong personality, and very understanding. Sandra... just doesn't care for me. She rags at me all the time. I think by now she hates me. Maybe she has good reason, but still.... Look Frank, I'm a human being. People think, oh, he's a dentist. They see a man in a white coat; they don't think, this is a real person. They don't see a real person. They see a dentist. His life revolves around teeth. No, it doesn't. I am a real person. I have feelings, I have emotions. I was young once. I'm still young, comparatively speaking. I still have a sex drive, God help me. I'm a living, breathing person. What's that line, if you tickle me, don't I laugh, if you cut me, don't I bleed? Something or other, by Shakespeare... was it the Merchant of Venice, or Othello? I can't remember, was it the Jewish guy, or the African guy. Oh, it doesn't matter."

"Caleb, I'm not going to pass judgment on you. I don't know Sandra. I barely know Charlotte. And you're right, it's none of my business."

"But you understand, don't you, why Charlotte would not be a good witness? In my malpractice case? This is my girlfriend. Who's going to believe a word she says?"

"She went with you to Portland."

"She did. Sandra doesn't know a thing about that. Yes. We went together."

"Can I get back to the money, Caleb: is it your money? There's all these rumors out there, I know rumors can be ridiculous, and they often are. But people are talking about blackmail.... This funny business with the money.... Whose money is it, Caleb? Maggie had it in a bank account. Why? Charlotte says it's her money. Do you know anything about it? What's the story, Caleb? Was Maggie supposed to deliver the money to somebody?"

"No, there's no blackmail, that's ridiculous, Frank. Look: I'll be honest with you... you're my lawyer, I know, everything I say to you, it's strictly confidential.... Here's the truth: I'm going to leave Sandra. I can't take it anymore. And I'm in love with Charlotte. I want to start a new life."

I said, "OK."

"Frank, I've got a chance now. A chance. It's what I want. A real life. I'm going to go off with Charlotte. But, and this is a deep dark secret, I need money. So I've sold my practice. My client list, my equipment, my lease of the office. I sold everything. To Dobbs. It's a lot of money, and he's paying it off gradually. And secretly. I insisted on that... and he knows why, so he's OK with it. He's paying it in installments, every month, he gives me a piece of what he owes me. That's the way I wanted it. It's all very hush-hush. I made him swear.... We have an agreement... Sandra doesn't know about it. Is what I'm doing illegal?"

"Illegal? No," I said, "but you're got to remember, this is a community property state, California is, I mean. Your income, it belongs to Sandra too. When you married her, did you have a prenup?"

"No.... I should have done that, but I just didn't think. You know, newlyweds, most of them, they're not thinking of money. Anyway, she's got money of her own, Sandra does. But would she have a claim to the value of my practice? I was a dentist long before I married Sandra, I had all of this, the equipment, well, most of it, some of it I bought later on, but the lease, it's a long-term lease; and the list of clients.... Do I owe her something?"

I actually didn't know the answer. Not on the tip of my tongue anyway. "I'm not sure she has a claim, or doesn't have a claim. Community property.... It can be technical. Do you want me to check it out, Caleb? I can do that for you."

He said: "Frank, I'm a desperate man. Maybe I'm cheating Sandra. I don't care. This is the way it's going to be. I don't want you to look anything up, because it doesn't make a damn bit of difference to me, and I don't honestly care what you find. I'm going ahead with this, and I don't care what she thinks. Or what she's entitled to."

"And Maggie? How did she get involved?"

He said, "Well, it was part of the plan. The secrecy part. Dobbs didn't care, he went along with the arrangement. I told Maggie all about it. She trusted me. We were good friends. She worked for me, for years. She knew about my troubles. The idea was, I'd get the money from Dobbs, in cash, and she'd put it in her bank account. Then after a while, I would get it from her, and put it in an account in the Cayman Islands. I'm going to go to Australia, Frank. Me and Charlotte. We'll start our new life there. I'm looking into what it takes to be a dentist in Australia. Melbourne, that's where we're going. I have a friend in Melbourne. I was there once, trip to Australia, with my first wife—we went snorkeling. I think I could make a life there."

I didn't know what to say. "This is risky business, Caleb."

"There's more," he said. "I've already made some arrangements.... I'm buying a practice in Melbourne, a dentist my friend knows, he's retiring. But I needed money upfront.... More than I was getting from Dobbs. And I did something which, I guess, isn't really ethical."

"Ethical?"

"Frank, I'm the executor of Dr. Sylvester's estate. Morris Sylvester. You know, he was my partner before Dobbs. A terrific dentist. But he was one of those people who don't really have a life. Never married. Lived with his mother, cranky old woman, but he was devoted to her. He was an only child. Well, she lived to be 98 or so. The last years, she was half-blind, and pretty feeble. He never went anywhere, just took care of her. I mean, he was here during the daytime, we got along just fine, sweet man, the patients liked him a lot. Well, he just worked and worked, and then he went home to that woman. Wish I had a son like that. I've got a daughter, she doesn't give a damn about me. Well, that's water under the bridge."

I had a feeling I knew where this was heading, as soon as he said the word: executor.

"You know," he said, "when the old bag finally died, I guess he felt, what was the point of going on with life. Most people don't know this, but he killed himself. Took a bunch of pills. No note or anything like that. Who would read it? Anyway, it was all hush-hush. He had quite a bit of money. His mother's, and then his. He never spent a dime on anything. And he didn't have any relatives, I mean, nobody close.... Some cousins in Cleveland, but they didn't mean a thing to him."

"He had a will? I gather he did," I said, "and he named you executor." I hate telling lies, but I didn't want to admit I had been poking around in the estate file of Morris Sylvester.

"Yes. Not a complicated estate. A few money gifts here and there. But the bulk of it, well, he left half of it to some dental charity, and the rest, in his mother's memory, to a society of people who grow some sort of flower, I don't remember which one, orchids, or hyacinths, or dahlias—I mean, who cares? In her day, his mother used to grow these flowers, in the house, and I guess this was her passion, more or less. Whatever. Anyway, I was in charge of the money, and... Frank, I know this is wrong, but I borrowed some money from the estate.... I had to. First of all, I need more upfront money, for the business in Melbourne. That was part of it. But then Charlotte needed some money, she really did. Some family thing. And I wanted to help her out, and I couldn't ask Sandra.... I know you're not supposed to do what I did. I'm going to pay it back. From the money I get from Dobbs."

"Caleb, let me tell you, as forcefully as I can, you absolutely must put that money back into that account. And right away. Just do it. This is really wrong, what you did, and it could get you in a lot of trouble...."

"I know you're right. I told Charlotte, I had to have the money back, and she agreed.... And I'll try to make amends, as soon as I can. But Frank, I can't do it right away. I just don't have the money. It's... well, it's gone into this account we have.... I need it, for Australia."

"You'll need it for San Quentin," I said. "Don't be a damn fool, Caleb. This is not a game. They'll take away your license. And maybe the news will get all the way to

Australia. Please, Caleb, I can't say this strongly enough: you have to replace the money."

I repeated this more than once. I was as emphatic as I could possibly be. Finally, he promised... at least he said he'd try. He hardly ate his meal. Of course, the man was troubled; any fool could see that. What a mess he had made of his life. The thought of it cast a pall over the table. When we left, I put my hand on his shoulder, and tried to cheer him up. "Caleb," I said. "I know you'll do the right thing. It'll turn out OK in the end."

He said: "I hope you're right."

I walked back to the office, deep in thought. Would he do the right thing? I couldn't be sure. Not really. He took money from an estate. He was cheating on his wife, with his dental assistant. Yet what, if anything, did these things have to do with Maggie's death? I was still groping for a motive. Maggie was handling money for Caleb Colegrove. She was warehousing the money until he needed it... or could shift it to the Cayman Islands, or whatever it was he was doing. Was that why she was killed?

And this notion that Caleb had, just possibly, been guilty of killing somebody.... I couldn't quite make sense of that either. And then there was Charlotte. She had told me a pack of lies, about the money. Now I more or less understood why. But what else was she lying about? She was not in the office that fatal morning. As far as we knew. Did that mean she couldn't have had a hand in Maggie's death?

I didn't go right back to my office. Instead, I walked around the block a few times, thinking and thinking. There was more to Caleb Colegrove than met the eye. I mean, what met the eye was a dentist. Caleb was right, we don't think of dentists as people. We think of them as dentists. I hope, if you're reading this and you're a dentist, that you don't take offense. It's not just dentists. It's the same with all sorts of people, I mean, people we see only in one narrow capacity. We don't think about the fact that they're people, that they have a life, a real life, outside of the office, the store, the street, or wherever you see them.

I took my car to the dealer the other day. I drive a Toyota. Six years old. I service it regularly. I see this guy, he's about 40, he's wearing greasy overalls, he's got a wrench in his hand, I can see the edge of a tattoo peeking out from his sleeve. He needs a shave. I don't spend one second thinking about him, all I care about is the car, how much is this costing me, are they doing a good job. But there's a private life there, isn't there? Not just work and the wrench and fixing cars, there's a life. There's a family. There's a home, of some sort. A sex life, I suppose. Dreams and ambitions. Likes and dislikes.

Or consider the plumber. We had a plumber come the other day. The toilet bowl was doing awful things; I'll spare you the disgusting details. Here he was, a young man, quite skinny, in a blue uniform, dirty blond hair, a nose slightly too big; he takes off his shoes at the door and puts on some sort of plastic booties. He too has a tiny bit of tattoo showing on his neck. His eyes were bloodshot, that's what I noticed. Spends every day on peoples' toilets and the like. But he too has a life. It's not all toilets and plumbing. And so it goes. The saleslady at Macy's, maybe 50 years old, overweight, too much makeup, with a ring on every single one of her fat and stubby fingers. Big bosoms. Dark rings under her eyes. Funny name, maybe Russian. She too. She has a life. All we usually think about is the sale, the big discount, and can she help Celia find her size? But then I wondered: where does she live? What does she do for kicks? Is she married or divorced? Is she happy? What diseases has she had? The point is: everybody has a story. Everybody.

And somebody's story, in this case, includes the commission of murder.

20

I only vaguely remember Morris Sylvester—a quiet man, somewhat overweight, a bit bald, very soft-spoken. Caleb was always my dentist, exclusively. But now I was intrigued by the decline and fall of the late Dr. Sylvester. I was dying to know more about his life, and, more especially, his death.

There was nowhere to turn except to Stanley—who, after all, had led me to look at the file for Dr. Sylvester's estate. I couldn't think of anybody else, except possibly Caleb and the people in the office, and I didn't want to do that, for obvious reasons.

I arranged to have coffee with Stanley. "What's up, Frank?" he said, when we were seated in a local Starbucks. The place was, as usual, filled with computer geeks, sipping their latte and staring at their laptops. We found a quiet corner.

"I want to talk about Dr. Morris Sylvester."

"Yeah? What about him? He's still dead, last time I checked."

"Spare me the sarcasm, Stanley. You told me to look at the papers in his estate, and I did. They were awfully interesting, as I'm sure you know. The will and the codicil. Very interesting. Made me wonder, among other things, about what killed the guy. What was the cause of death?"

"What killed him? How did he die? You say that, as if there's some big surprise coming. You know, we're all going to die. Morris went first. That's the way it is sometimes."

"Come on, Stanley," I said. "Don't be such a jerk. Caleb said, he killed himself. Swallowed a bunch of pills."

"So they say."

"Stanley: is it possible that wasn't the whole story? Is it possible somebody killed him? And made it look like suicide?"

"You've been reading too many novels, Frank."

"This is real life, Stanley. I know people said it was suicide. But are you absolutely sure about the suicide?"

"Well, look, Frank, what else? I wasn't there. They said he killed himself."

"People who commit suicide usually leave a note, Stanley. Was there a note? Caleb said there wasn't."

"Well, he was wrong. There was a note. Caleb never saw it. I didn't either. But I heard about it, from his doctor, the one that signed the death certificate."

"What did it say?"

"I don't know exactly. It was typed on a computer. I guess it said, I don't want to go on living or some such thing. The usual. The guy was completely broken up, about his mother. Wretched old bitch. I thought she would live forever. But she finally died. Had cancer, heart trouble, emphysema, dementia, you name it. Morris was totally attached to her though. When she died, I think he felt, this is the end for me. Nothing to live for, blah blah."

"A typewritten note, you said."

"On the computer."

"Couldn't that be a fake? Anybody can type something, it's not like a handwritten note."

"God, Frank, what's gotten into you? The man committed suicide. Let him rest in peace. Anyway, why would anybody want to kill the guy? A lonely, unattractive bachelor dentist. Not your usual victim."

"Money," I said.

"What are you talking about?"

"Stanley," I said, "the man left behind a very nice

estate. Eight million, ten, I'm not sure of the amount. You probably know. People kill people for a lot less, in case you weren't aware of that."

"Right," he said. "The money. A member of Dentists Without Borders, fresh from doing root canal work in Nepal, creeps into his house, and stuffs a fatal dose of pills down his throat. No: wait: it wasn't that guy at all. It was a member of the local dahlia society. Those flower-lovers, look out. They can be murderous. Remember, they're the only two beneficiaries that really were going to get a big pile of dough, if Morris Sylvester left planet Earth."

"So you think it's absurd, what I'm saying."

"Absurd is the word. Yes," Stanley said. "Unless you have something else in mind."

"No, I don't," I said. Which wasn't true. The something else I had in mind was Caleb Colegrove. Caleb needed money. Maybe he knew about the will, which left him everything, but not the codicil, which left him nothing. And then there was that mysterious statement from Maggie. I was beginning to think I saw some daylight—the proverbial light at the end of the tunnel. The lights all pointed in the same direction: toward Caleb Colegrove.

This was bothersome. My dentist? A killer? And could I prove this? No. Absolutely not. And I had no idea where to turn to for answers... and how. Inside my head, too, I kept hearing Celia's voice, telling me to mind my own business and stick to the practice of law.

I wanted to disobey, but I didn't know how.

21

I was surprised to find Zelda in my office, when I came back from lunch the next day.

"Frank," she said, stretching her long legs out in front of her, "I've become an addict. Not drugs, but murder. And not any old murder, but this one. I never knew a murder victim before. And now, it's Maggie. I can't work, my new novel, it's just hanging in thin air. I'm spending all my time thinking about this case. Milo is such a sweetheart... he's very supportive. But skeptical. I told him, honey, I can't help myself."

What could I say?

"I know you're working on it, too, Frank. Remember, we're partners. We're in this together."

"Zelda," I said, "I swear to you, I am not, repeat not, working on this case. I did agree to do a few things for Maggie's daughter. And I'm doing them. But... you know, we've got a police force in this town. I'm sure they're working hard to solve this thing. Maybe we should just leave it to them."

She dismissed the police with a wave of her hands. "Oh, the police. They're incompetent. Listen: I have two theories, Frank, and I want to check them out with you. OK?"

I made a feeble protest. Actually, I was curious to know what her theories were... and how she arrived at them.

"You know what my first theory is? It's Xyloquex. It's

that company across the street. You know, it's really creepy, it's supposed to be some sort of business, they claim to be consultants of some kind... but the door is usually locked, and there's nobody there during the day...."

"That's not exactly true," I said. "There's a kid, Judd, I met him. He works there, he's some sort of gofer. And then there's the head of the company, president or whatever, Werner Brown; he's been a patient of Dr. Colegrove. And there's some sort of receptionist or secretary. So there's people there."

"Sometimes there are. I saw this Judd," she said. "A complete moron. Like most of the people his age nowadays. Probably spends his spare time on some ridiculous video game. Head full of sawdust. He wouldn't know what was going on there, if it hit him in the face. Maybe I shouldn't complain. The women who read my novels, well, the less said about them the better. Anyway: did you know, I talked about that place, with Maggie? We talked about Xyloquex."

"No, I didn't know."

"I was writing my vampire book. I was having a little bit of writer's block. Milo said, sweetheart, take the day off. I was at the dentist, and then I went to the coffee shop, and Maggie was on her break. I said, sit down, let's talk. I can't remember who brought up the subject of Xyloquex, but I told her I was writing a book about vampires... anyway, about the company, I said, half-joking, maybe the people there are vampires. They can't stand daylight. Maggie didn't find it funny, I don't know. Odd reaction. She got all huffy, I never saw her like that, almost angry, she said, that's ridiculous, Zelda. It's just a company. People work there. I didn't pay much attention at the time, but now.... Don't you see? I brought up the vampires again, and Maggie... she changed the subject. She knew something. Something fishy is going on there. Not vampires, but something else. And Maggie knew what it was. She just wasn't talking."

"And what do you think it was?"

"I don't know. But don't you see: Maggie isn't around, they shut her up. She knew too much. I heard a rumor, they're a front for some organization, Blackacre or some name like that, it hires mercenaries, people who fight wars in Africa. Milo said to me, be careful, honeybun. Those companies, they're ruthless, they're dangerous. And it's all very hush-hush. I think the government is mixed up in it, but it could be something top secret. Mercenaries. Oh, yes, and they buy weapons, you know, guns, bazookas, missiles, whatever. They have these wars all over Africa. So I think Maggie knew what they were doing, and of course it's completely illegal. Those people will stop at nothing."

"Zelda," I said, "why would a company like that have an office here? In San Mateo? Next door to a bunch of orthodontists, Chinese restaurants, and places that do hot yoga? I mean, be serious."

"Why not? It's just the place to hide. Nobody would suspect a thing. Suburbia, you know; everything seems so harmless. They had those Russian moles in New Jersey, just ordinary folks, living in the burbs. For all you know, I'm a Russian spy myself."

"If so, you're wasting your time talking to me," I said. "I haven't got anything the Russians could conceivably be interested in."

"I had another idea," she said. "Drones."

"Drones?"

"I'm thinking, Xyloquex. Maybe they have some machines in there, you know, the ones that send off the drones."

"But Zelda, really," I said. "Does that make any sense? The Pentagon is in charge of the drones. Or the CIA or something. I mean, they're not sending off drones from San Mateo, California, as I said, you know, a place full of orthodontists and Chinese restaurants."

"Why not? It's perfect cover. You think you need an

airfield? No, you don't. You just sit in front of a computer, and you push a button, you've got a screen—meanwhile, there's a terrorist in Pakistan, he's riding in a jeep, and the drone kills him, just like that. Kills a lot of other people, too. Actually, I think it's scandalous; Milo thinks so too. We're pacifists. But let's not talk politics. And by the way, you keep mentioning Chinese restaurants: I've got my suspicion about at least one of those Chinese restaurants."

I too had suspicions. I suspect that one or two of them use MSG and make my head buzz. But Zelda had something quite different in mind. "One of those restaurants, you know, the one down the street, across from the bank, it's called 'Dragonseed,' did you ever go in there, Frank? There's never anybody there. Oh, maybe two or three people. I went in there once, the waiter didn't speak a word of English. I ordered something, I pointed to it on the menu, but it took them half an hour to bring me the food. The place was almost totally empty, and they took half an hour and you just know they're not exactly making it from scratch. So I used to wonder, how do they stay in business? Well: maybe they stay in business because Chinese food really isn't what they're doing, it's just a front."

"Zelda, with all due respect, I just don't believe that. A front for what?"

"Money laundering? Human trafficking? Who knows? You think it's just my imagination? But these days, anything is possible. Milo says, the way things are going, the only people who hit the nail on the head are people who are paranoid. Anyway, Frank: I'll grant you, this Chinese restaurant is probably kosher. I'm not talking about the food. I mean, they're not some sort of front for crime. But that Xyloquex Corporation. Mark my words...."

Was this the best Zelda could come up with?

I did feel that there was something mysterious about the Xyloquex company. But, as I told Zelda, there was nothing concrete to connect them with Maggie's death.

"Oh, isn't there?" she said. "Then why did Maggie go there? Because she did go there. We know that. Why? I waited out in front of the place, at around five o'clock. I wasn't going to get anything out of that moron, Judd. But then there was Barbara...."

"Barbara? Which Barbara? I know lots of Barbaras."

"The one at Xyloquex. Sort of a receptionist. Answers the phone and so on. Woman of about 40. Wears much too much make-up, dyes her hair some ridiculous color. I managed to catch her, coming out of the place. I said, can I ask you some questions? She said, who the hell are you? It wasn't easy to pin her down. I showed her a picture of Maggie, I got it from her daughter. I said, do you recognize this woman? She said, of course I do, she's the one that got herself killed in the dentist's office, her picture was in the paper. I said, no, I mean, did you ever see her in your office? She said, what's it to you, and so on. But finally she said, maybe just to get rid of me, yes, she came by a few times. What for? I asked. She said, how should I know? She was bringing something to somebody. What was she bringing, and for who? She said, listen, I can't stand here all day, I'm late for an appointment, and off she went."

It wasn't much. But it did connect Maggie with Xyloquex. For what purpose, we still had no idea. But Zelda seemed eager to continue: "I'll get to the bottom of this," she said. I wished her good luck. I never found out any other theories. Not that time, anyway.

22

Later on, in the afternoon, I decided to take a break, walk around the block, get a little sunshine. I had been working on a document for a client and I was bored silly. As I got to the corner, I saw Judd. He was sitting on a bench, eating a cheeseburger and french fries. He had a can of Coke in front of him.

"Hey, Judd, you got a minute?"

He gave me a fishy stare. I guess he recognized me. "Yeah, what about?"

"This company you work for: exactly, what does it do? I mean, you're there every day, what are they up to? The name doesn't tell us very much."

"Man, look, I can't tell you. I mean, it's not a secret, it's just, it's big science, something about the genome, whatever that is. That's what I think. Hey, I'm just a kind of a gofer there, you know? I needed a job, any kind of job, I'm broke.... I owe people money.... I bought stuff, and I'm having trouble paying for it. You know what I'm saying?"

"It's hard to find work these days," I said, trying to sound sympathetic.

"Don't I know it. Hey, I was unemployed, believe me, it's tough. All these places, they want references and stuff. I did some bad stuff in high school, and man, it makes it really hard to get anything. I couldn't even get a job at Walmart, I thought they take anybody, that's what somebody told me, but they don't."

I had no interest in Walmart's hiring policies. I tried to steer the conversation back to Xyloquex. I asked him: "Well, who runs the place?"

"Nobody, really... most of the time, nobody's there at all. This guy Werner, he comes in sometimes. He's the manager or something. He tells me what to do. Then there's this lady, Barbara, she handles the mail and stuff. She's there most of the time. Really fresh, nasty bitch, if you want my opinion. Always ordering me around. The owner, I never seen him at all. I don't even know his name. He's not here. He's always in Aba Daba, I think that's the name, some place in Arabia or whatever."

"Hey, Judd, maybe they're doing something secret? For the government?"

"You think? Anyway, who cares? But what's it to you? Like I said, I was broke, I needed a job. My mom... never mind. I wanted to move in with her, I couldn't pay the rent at the place I was living, but you think she wants me hanging around? No way. She's only got one bedroom, and I'd be sleeping on a couch. Not that I'd like that, but man, I'm getting desperate. Maybe I could live with a bunch of guys or something. And I need something that pays better than this place. Maybe I could get a job in construction, they make good money. It's hard to break in though. Unions and stuff. And they're all Mexican, I think you got to be Mexican to get a job. I don't know, maybe.... Anyway, my mom's got a boyfriend now, she doesn't want me hanging around."

His fingers were all greasy from the fried potatoes. He licked at them, then dabbed at his fingers with a paper napkin. "You work around here," he said, "if you hear of something, let me know." A clock struck somewhere. He jumped up suddenly and said: "Jesus, I'm late. That bitch will kill me." He crumpled up the wrapping from his cheeseburger and fries, threw it down on the sidewalk and dashed off.

I couldn't imagine hearing of a job Judd would be qualified to fill. He seemed like a total loser.

I sat on the bench for a while, thinking. I faced not one, but three mysteries. Were they connected? The first was the death of poor Maggie. There was the strange case of the late Dr. Sylvester. And then there was Xyloquex.

23

I had called Werner Brown at Xyloquex a number of times, with no results. A woman—this was, I suppose, the "bitch, Barbara"—answered the phone and promised, in a frosty voice, to take a message. "What is this concerning?" she asked. I could hardly be honest with her. I said I was an attorney, and I had a legal matter to discuss. She was persistent: "What sort of matter?" I said, "I prefer not to specify at the moment, but please give Mr. Brown this message and my phone number. Tell him I would like to see him, if possible. My office is just across the street from your company. He can come here, or I can go there."

Somewhat to my surprise, she called back, said Mr. Brown would be happy to see me, and we fixed a time; he would prefer (she said) my office, rather than his. Now, here he was, sitting across from me, in the flesh. He introduced himself before sitting down. I noticed a slight accent. He was a Swiss citizen, he told me. Did he look Swiss? I have no idea what looking Swiss might mean. Werner Brown, at any rate, was middle aged; he had a hooked nose, thin lips, and bloodshot eyes. He had a way of moving his head slightly, up and down, a kind of nervous tic. His hair was thin, receding, nondescript in color, maybe you could call it one of the fifty shades of gray. When he bent over, I could see a bald spot in the middle of his skull. I couldn't quite identify the accent. "Brown" didn't strike me as a Swiss name. Maybe he changed his name, or altered it from whatever name he was born with.

"You're the president of the Xyloquex Corporation, aren't you?"

"Not the president. That's not the title I use."

"What then?"

"Does it matter? I don't see why it matters. Yes, I work for the company. That is quite right. In what capacity, I'd rather not say. How does this concern you?"

Of course, it didn't concern me at all. I was simply curious to know more about the mysterious Xyloquex company. I couldn't think of a good way to bring it into the conversation. I certainly wasn't going to tell him that at least one person thought they were directing small, deadly drones... or acting as some kind of criminal front.

"You know why I'm here, I suppose," he said. "They told me you were investigating the case of this woman, this Maggie person. Of course I had nothing to do with it. I barely knew the woman. I only saw her when I visited the dentist. But I realize, because I was a patient, because I was supposed to come to the office that day, that makes me... I won't say a suspect.... But someone who the authorities would certainly want to question. And they did. You surely know, of course, that I already spoke to the police? I told them everything I know, which is absolutely nothing. You're acting, I suppose, as a private investigator. Can I ask who hired you?"

"I'm not a private investigator," I said. "I'm not an investigator at all. I did promise to, uh, talk to people."

"You promised? Who did you promise? Was it that woman who spoke to me, the daughter?"

"Yes, it was. I'm... just doing her a favor."

"It's a very peculiar favor," he said. "Unheard of. I thought seriously about simply ignoring your call. Not coming here at all. This would never happen in Switzerland: private individuals, meddling into official police affairs."

I could see this was going badly. Usually, I would

shrivel up into a small, prune-like being, and give up. But somehow, Werner Brown touched a nerve. He seemed so arrogant. The secrecy, the haughty tone of voice: he simply irritated me. His obnoxious manner somehow emboldened me. Abruptly, I stopped defending myself, and went right back to the topic he wanted to avoid.

"I'm sure the Swiss do things better than we do. Maybe your business is owed by a Swiss corporation? Your business—I mean, the Xyloquex Corporation. You never told me what they do, what they make, you know, that sort of thing."

"Really, Mr. May, it's none of your business."

"I know that. But... there's something odd going on here, isn't there? Most businesses, they're eager to tell us what they do, they spend money on advertising, so.... I was just curious, that's all."

"Just curious? I'm afraid you'll have to remain curious."

Rebuffed again, I dropped the subject. Instead I asked, "Why were you going to see the dentist?"

"What a question. The usual reason. Teeth."

"What was the matter with your teeth?"

"Nothing."

"Nothing? Then why were you seeing the dentist?"

He seemed annoyed. "That must be obvious. I come regularly. I am very careful about my teeth. Teeth are important, as I'm sure you know. I have my teeth cleaned, checked. Quite regularly. Usually, with this woman, Charlotte. Occasionally, the other one, Estelle. Sometimes they take X-rays. The office is nearby, which makes it very convenient. A great saving in time. I must say, frankly, I had made up my mind, not to go there again, to use a different dentist. But I didn't cancel this particular appointment."

"You were going to change dentists? Can I ask you why?"

"Now that too is none of your business: how I choose

dentists. Let's just say, I was fed up with something going on there."

"Something going on? In Dr. Colegrove's office? May I ask what it was?"

"You may ask... but I don't care to answer."

I could see that Werner Brown had no intention of enlightening me. On this or anything else. But I kept trying: "Did you know Maggie, the woman who was killed?"

"The Communist?"

"Communist?"

"I don't mean that literally. She was not a card-carrying member of the Communist Party, no. I wonder if there is such a thing anymore, here in the United States. No, not a member. But she had that mindset. Government should do everything, run everything, plan everything, own everything. It's appalling that people like her have the right to vote. There are far too many of such people. People who don't live in the modern world. They don't realize the game has changed. The new dentist, Dobbs, is more of a realist."

"So you're switching from Colegrove to Dobbs?"

"I may do that. I was going to go elsewhere entirely, but that was before the unfortunate incident. Before that woman died. I wanted to avoid her, and that slut Charlotte; I was going to go in that morning, and ask for Estelle. But of course you know what happened."

"Charlotte wasn't there that morning, anyway," I said.

"She wasn't?"

"No. That's what I was told. Maggie was there, and Dr. Colegrove; and that other assistant. Nobody else, as far as I know."

"Then how come I originally had an appointment with this Charlotte creature?"

I shrugged my shoulders. "No idea."

He said. "Maybe she was there after all, hiding in

some closet and some vacant office, with Colegrove. You know they were having sex, don't you? He's a married man, but of course who cares about that, these days? Maybe she's married too; I wouldn't doubt it. I saw them once, together, misbehaving. They didn't think I saw anything, but he was squeezing her bottom. A man like that, he has no self-control."

"I don't see the relevance...."

"Don't you? Maybe that woman, that Maggie, maybe she was going to tell his wife. Moralistic bitch that she was. So he killed her. I told Dobbs, he should get out of there. The atmosphere is poisonous. Downright poisonous. Start your own practice, I told him. Take a risk; and I think he listened to me. He's ambitious, Dobbs, clear-headed, and hard-working. Kind of person this country needs. Believes in getting ahead on your own, not sniveling and begging and waiting for a handout."

Where was this going? I listened to his screed for a while, asked him a few questions about what happened that morning; and learned little or nothing. What really fascinated me was his statement that something was "going on" at the Colegrove office. Was he referring only to sex between Caleb and Charlotte? But Brown didn't strike me as puritanical. He called Maggie a "moralistic bitch." Presumably he, Brown, was not moralistic.

I couldn't let go. I said, "Mr. Brown, you said something was 'going on' in that office. I don't think you meant Colegrove's sex life. It might be important to know what you did mean."

"It might be," he said. "And I have, in fact, mentioned certain things to the police. But why should I mention them to you?"

I had no answer. He got up to go. "If you had talked to me about what was going on a month ago," he said. "I would have said: ask Maggie. Ask her why she comes to my office. Ask her what the point of it is."

"Mr. Brown," I said, "she's dead. I can't ask her."

"You think I don't know that? Then ask Charlotte. Not that she'll tell you the truth."

And then he was gone.

24

Helen called me the next day. I was embarrassed; I had really very little to report. I couldn't say I had made much progress. Naturally, I wasn't going to tell her about Zelda's wild ideas. I would leave that to Zelda.

Helen was very disappointed. She said, "I know mother's dead, and I can't bring her back. And, yes, I want to know who killed her; and I'd like to see that person punished, but I'm not vindictive, I'm just not that kind of person. I just need... it's because of all these rumors. I know my mother was a wonderful, kind, loving woman. All this talk, funny money, blackmail, it's so upsetting to me. That's why I want to know what happened. I just know, my mother never did anything wrong, anything bad, she wouldn't hurt a fly, she wouldn't cheat anybody. I just know that, Frank. That's what I want to show. I don't want this cloud over her memory."

I had the feeling she was on the verge of tears. I asked her: "Did your mother talk to you very much about, well, things at work? Stuff that was going on, in the dentist's office?"

"Not much, really. I mean, there wasn't that much to talk about. I assumed nothing was going on, I mean, nothing worth talking about. I used to tell her about my kids, she was interested, what gramma isn't, and I would tell her my troubles, and I'd ask her about her health, you know, how the arthritis was going. Well, once in a while she'd mention something about the office. You know, she just loved Dr. Colegrove. She really did. And she liked the old man, Dr. Sylvester, she felt so sorry for him. She used to tell me, he needs a wife, poor thing. Especially after his mother died. And I said, well, mother, do you need a husband? And she said, God forbid, why would I want to get together with some old man. No, good heavens, you're not thinking about Morris Sylvester? I said, no, no, mother, of course not. Actually, I was thinking about it, in a way. Mother would never have married him. I think she was finished with that stuff. I think she felt, enough is enough."

"You said she loved Dr. Colegrove. That's the word you used: loved."

"Oh, Frank, don't get me wrong. She felt motherly toward him. Things were different, though, after Dr. Sylvester died, poor soul. That new doctor, the partner, Dobbs, oh, that's something else. She really didn't like him. In a big way. And they were always arguing, arguing. She told me that. He was just not nice. It poisoned the whole atmosphere."

"Was it politics they argued about?"

"Yes. Politics. Can you imagine? I don't think it was mother that brought up politics. No, it was Dobbs. He was this awful right-wing person, I mean, to the right of Attila the Hun. He kept talking about this woman writer, Ann Rand, or whatever her name was, and he just couldn't keep his opinions to himself. Or maybe it was Paul Rand. I can't remember. Something she wrote or he wrote about an architect or whatever. I guess it was propaganda, and this Dr. Dobbs, he swallowed it. He was just plain mean. He was always after my mother, criticizing her. He saw that she got checks from Social Security, I mean, thank God for that, she earned it, didn't she? He hated Social Security, and Medicare; he said, people like you, you're parasites. That's the exact word he used: parasites."

She broke off, and I could tell that she was crying. She was saying things like "poor mother," and mentally I handed her a Kleenex. She got a grip on herself and went on: "He said that to her, bold as brass, you're a parasite. There's two kinds of people in this country. Makers and takers. Honestly, that's the phrase he used. You people, you're takers. You're sucking the blood out of this country. Mother was hurt and angry. A parasite, imagine. The woman worked and worked her whole life. Of course, the reason why he picked on her, mother was a Democrat, dyed in the wool Democrat, she worked for the party, you know, at election times, she used to stuff envelopes, make phone calls, they had phone banks, and she would call people, ask them to vote for the party. She was very active; and he knew it. I mean, it was obvious, she wore Obama buttons, and she didn't make a secret out of what she did. Dr. Colegrove didn't care. I don't think he was interested in politics. But this guy, Ryan Dobbs... well, the two of them, they had ferocious arguments."

I thought to myself: two right-wingers—Werner Brown and Ryan Dobbs. Here, in the San Francisco Bay Area, we just don't have that many Republicans, especially ones on the far right. Around here, they're an endangered species. The Bay Area is full of people who fled places like Mississippi for dear life.

I said to her: "You don't think Dobbs killed her, do you? For political reasons?"

"No... I don't think so.... I hope not.... But everybody else loved mother. Really. You wouldn't believe the notes I've gotten, condolence cards. People I never met. The other women, Estelle, Chloe, they said such sweet things about mother. And Dr. Colegrove, he sent the most beautiful flowers, they must have cost a lot of money. I even got a note from her podiatrist. Mother used to go to a podiatrist, she had these pains with her toes, and ingrown toenails, you should see the note he sent, personal note, it made me cry. That's what I mean, Frank, everybody loved her. Why did this happen to her? And why are people saying all these things?"

"Helen," I said, "you're right, it would be good to find out what happened. I knew your mother, and I agree with you, a hundred percent. She was a good person. I don't like Dobbs, myself. But I don't think he's violent. I mean, this country is full of lunatics of one sort of another; that's true enough. But I don't think Dobbs is that kind of lunatic. It's all talk, in my opinion. I know, you never can tell. But really.... After all, he's a dentist."

She said: "I know, I know. But... dentists.... Why do you think a dentist couldn't kill somebody? I like my own dentist, but you have to wonder. Aren't they a little bit, well, sadistic? Drilling people's teeth, or actually pulling them out. That's why they go into the business, they know they're going to inflict pain on people. I said to mother, I'm glad you have a good job, I could never work in a dentist's office, I'm scared to death of dentists—I have to take a pill to calm me down before I go, and I break out in a sweat. My dentist, Angus, he said to me, Helen, are you really that frightened? And I was. I think this Dr. Dobbs is a vicious, vicious person. Truly evil. Why would somebody do a thing like this? It has to be some kind of maniac. And believe me, Dr. Dobbs...."

But I just couldn't see Ryan Dobbs as a homicidal maniac. I told her that.

"Oh, I'm sure you're right. But there's something sinister about him. Really. And I think he's connected with that company across the street, Xyloquex, isn't that the name? Nobody knows who or what it's all about, and I think it's something political."

"Dr. Dobbs is connected with the company? How do you know that?"

"I talked to this woman. She's really making an effort.... That tall woman, Zelda...." (I thought: oh my God, not her.).

"This Zelda," she went on, "is really working on this thing. Oh, Frank, I don't mean to insult you. I know you're trying hard. It's not a competition. The more the merrier. I just have to get to the bottom of this. Somehow I don't think mother will rest in peace, until we get some answers. I won't, that's for sure."

"What does Zelda say?" I asked, in all innocence.

"I wish you'd talk to her," she said. "Zelda has so many ideas!"

I told her I'd be happy to talk to Zelda, and I told her, because I thought honesty was the best policy at this point, that I had already been in contact with her. "Oh, I'm so glad," Helen said. I didn't add that I thought Zelda's ideas verged on lunacy. I asked, "Did she tell you what the connection was, I mean, between Dobbs and that company?"

"Not really," Helen said. "I think she was working on it."

I had been hoping that if I dawdled long enough, Zelda would lose her zeal and the whole thing might go away. But I was wrong. Zelda called me on the phone. "We need a conference," she said. "We have to put our heads together." There was nothing I fancied less than putting my head together with Zelda, but she was a woman who never took no for an answer—that much was clear.

We met in a coffee shop. She ordered a nonfat, decaf latte. "Lots of milk," she said. "Milo is lactose intolerant," she said to me, "so when I'm out on my own, I have as much dairy as I possibly can. Cheese, yogurt, you name it. OK: I'm rambling. Let's get back to the subject. What's your current theory, Frank?"

"Zelda, I don't really have one."

"Oh, but I know you do. I can tell just by looking at you. You're shrewd; you keep things tightly managed. Lawyers are usually shrewd. They learn that in law school. How to be shrewd. My second husband was a lawyer. He was extremely shrewd, on money matters, anyway.... Did you know I was married three times? First the furrier, then the lawyer, and now Milo. Well, that's neither here nor there. What I'm wondering is: are you saying you don't have a theory, because you don't, or because you don't want to share things with me? I can accept that, Frank. I'm a big girl. That's OK. Me, I'm willing to share everything I have."

I thought the best thing to do was simply keep quiet and listen.

"You know," she said. "I think, very likely, this is a political crime. Yes, a political crime. You know about Dobbs, don't you? These people can be dangerous. They have no moral sense. Maggie was very vulnerable, and she was a liberal. But that's just one theory. I think maybe it was a political crime in a deeper sense. Maybe a rehearsal for something much bigger. You think this is just a little something, an old woman in a dentist's office. No, there's something really significant going on here. This company, Xyloquex... they're at the bottom of it, I'm sure."

"Why do you think so, Zelda?"

"A hunch... Intuition... I could be wrong.... What do you think?"

"Really, Zelda, I just don't see this as political. Or drones or whatever. Maybe I'm just naïve, or conventional."

"You're probably right," she said. "Actually, I have a better theory. It's Dr. Colegrove himself."

"He killed Maggie? But why, Zelda?"

"It's all tied up with the trip to Oregon. Allegedly to go to some dental convention or whatever. And Dobbs is involved.... Dr. Dobbs, you know, Colegrove's partner.

"What about him?"

"The trip to Oregon. You know about it. Dobbs went, and he had a thing with some woman, did you know that? He picked her up in a bar. She had an accident, and she's suing."

"I do know about it."

"Well: that woman, who seduced him, this was all planned in advance, believe it or not. She just happened to see him, in a bar? No way. She was an investigator, there's more here than meets the eye. She was really checking out Colegrove; she was trying to get to him through Dobbs. I absolutely know that's true. I told Milo and he said, honey, you're a genius. You could be a private eye."

"The woman was an investigator?" I had heard from Ryan Dobbs that she was, but I really didn't know what that meant.

"Absolutely. An insurance company is after Colegrove. Erewhon Insurance Company. I know that too. He's in deep trouble. I think that Colegrove knows they're closing in on him. I think he's been paying off Maggie, that's where she got the money from, this mysterious money. Isn't this exciting? I haven't had such fun in years. It's a real high. I love excitement. Did you know I had an affair once with a man from UPS? He came to the door, you know, in that brown uniform, I love brown uniforms. He was delivering a tea kettle I ordered from Amazon. I spent the weekend with him, in Carmel. He was married, too. But I didn't care. I was reckless. Don't worry: it was after the lawyer, but before Milo. Anyway, that's my hunch. Colegrove was paying off Maggie. And he got tired of it, tired of the blackmail. So he got rid of her."

"You can't be serious, Zelda. Dr. Colegrove? Killing his receptionist, in cold blood? Tell me you're not serious."

"Frank, I'm completely serious. Or maybe it was partly an accident; they were quarreling, and he hit her, and.... I don't have any proof. Not yet. I think Dobbs knows. I'm hot on the trail."

I said, "Zelda, Colegrove wouldn't kill Maggie. They were friends. He was very fond of her. And she was devoted to him. That's what her daughter says. And I think it's true."

She paused, and played with her teaspoon. She said: "Maybe you're right, Frank. I should listen to you. I should trust you. Maybe you have better judgment than I do. It's your name: Frank. I believe in names. Milo fell in love with me because I was a Zelda. And, by the way, the man from UPS, do you know, his name was Frank, too."

"The world is full of Franks," I said, somewhat embarrassed.

"He was so erotic," she said. "And he didn't even realize it. Like you, Frank. I just loved to unbutton his shirt. He used to say, Zelda, I'm working, I can't do this. It didn't last. And then I met Milo. I never saw this Frank again. He was an inspiration though. I got a terrific idea from him, for a novel. This driver, he's got a truck, brown truck. He's delivering packages, but really, he's a serial killer. Nobody notices a delivery truck. He carries a package, knocks on the door, when somebody answers, he kills them. What do you think, Frank? Does it have possibilities?"

"I thought you wrote romances, Zelda."

"I did, I did. But I'm branching out. I told you, the romance market is so crowded. Milo encouraged me. You remember, we thought about vampires, zombies, whatever. The trouble with these romance novels, you had to do research, so boring.... I mean, what were pirates really like, what kind of ships they had, what they wore. And you had to look up the history of Barbados and god knows what else, I just got tired of all that. I mean, most people don't care, but I wanted to be so accurate. And if you're not, somebody calls you on it; I've had that experience once too often, thank you."

She loved to talk. "I'm going to do more investigating," she said. "I'm not shy. Tall people aren't shy, did you know that? I'm very tall. I used to play women's basketball, believe it or not."

And then suddenly she said: "Charlotte."

"Charlotte? What about Charlotte?"

"I'm suspicious of her too. You did know about her and Colegrove."

"Yes," I said, "I knew."

"Maybe lots of people knew. Maggie knew. The wife didn't know. But don't you think, this is suspicious?"

"Suspicious? How? What on earth would it have to do with Maggie?"

"Ah! Maybe nothing," she said.

"But tell me, Zelda, you said Dobbs had something to do with Xyloquex. How do you know that?"

"Just a guess. I heard something from Felicity... you know, the woman in the coffee shop. The waitress. The one with the hairspray. She knew Maggie. I had a long talk with Felicity. She loved talking about the case. She's never been so close to a real mystery story, she said. Anyway, she said Dobbs and Brown, the executive from Xyloquex, they had coffee together once. Sat in a booth."

"That's a fairly thin connection," I said.

"Connections start out thin," she said. "And then they get thicker."

After that she left.

25

There were so many theories, so many angles, that I could get dizzy just thinking about them. As yet, I just couldn't connect the dots. Nothing cohered. But there were plenty of dots, so to speak. The mysterious money. Xyloquex. Colegrove and Charlotte. The right-wing dentist, Ryan Dobbs. The late Morris Sylvester, and his estate. There were more questions than answers; but I did have a vague feeling, somewhere deep inside my brain, that I was making progress.

And at least I was able to clear up one of the minor mysteries. This happened when I was at lunch. Lunches seemed to figure significantly in this business, in some odd way. So much seems to turn on where I ate lunch, and with whom.

I had decided to try Dragonseed, the Chinese restaurant Zelda was suspicious of. Not that I shared her suspicions. I'm always on the lookout for another good Chinese restaurant. When I came in, I saw Caleb Colegrove, sitting alone in a booth.

"Can I join you?"

"Oh yes, Frank, of course."

There were only a handful of customers. Could Zelda be right that this was some sort of front, and not a serious restaurant? But as it turned out, there was another, perfectly good explanation for the problems of Dragonseed: the food was terrible. But I couldn't know this at the time. Nor could Caleb.

"How are you, Caleb?" I asked, after the waiter took our order.

"Awful. How else could I be? This whole business... I wish the police would arrest somebody and get it over with. A drug addict, or somebody crazy, who just broke in, and poor Maggie just happened to be in the wrong place at the wrong time. It's the thing I want more than anything else. You can't imagine what a strain all this is. And it's... it's interfering with my plans. I want so desperately to get away, start a new life. Me and Charlotte. I'd like a family, too.... My own daughter is like a stranger to me...."

"I don't want to be indelicate," I said, "but isn't Charlotte a little, well, a little old to think of children?"

"She's 45. It's not impossible," he said.

I said nothing. "Oh, I know," he said, "there's issues of fertility. And risk. Older mothers, yes, it's riskier. But did you know, it's less risky if you've given birth before? And Charlotte has given birth."

I vaguely remembered that Charlotte had said something about a child before. So I nodded my head. But I could see, from the look on his face, that he felt he had said something he hadn't really meant to say, something that just slipped out. I added quickly, "I don't mean to pry." Of course, I did mean to pry. I just couldn't admit it.

He hesitated. Then he said, "Well, it's not something she likes to talk about. No, she doesn't have children. Now. But yes, she had a child. Years ago. It lived a few months, and then died, of something. I don't know what. She doesn't like to talk about it. Then when she got married.... Her husband, he didn't want children. She got pregnant once, had an abortion. So... she feels this sense of loss, it's always been a very sore subject. Nobody knows this story, not the details. I never bring it up with Charlotte. I know she'd like to have a baby, start a family. Even at this late date."

I couldn't help asking: "Did Maggie... know about

Charlotte's... secret?"

He smiled. "Maggie. She knew everybody's secrets. People told Maggie everything. Maggie was very understanding, very empathetic, poor woman—somebody you could trust, somebody who could keep your secret. I was glad Charlotte had somebody she could talk to. I couldn't talk to her. Not on that subject. I think she was haunted by the memory of her dead child. What would it have been like, you know, when it grew up, that sort of thing."

You had to wonder. Did Maggie know too many secrets? Something it was dangerous to know, and it ended up killing her?

The food came, and I tried to eat it. Caleb did the same. We agreed: this was definitely sub-par. We chatted about restaurants for a while. Caleb liked Indian food, he said, and recommended a couple of local eateries. "And there's a terrific Afghan restaurant... have you ever tried Afghan food?" I hadn't.

Meanwhile, I was thinking over the things Caleb had told me. Something didn't quite compute. Charlotte had mentioned a son. According to Caleb, the son was dead. The way Charlotte mentioned him, it didn't seem as if he was dead. Was he lying, was she lying, or what?

After we had dissected a number of restaurants, I felt bold enough to ask a question that had been on my mind. It was about Stanley. What was Stanley doing at the office, that morning—the fateful morning? I asked Caleb point blank. At first he tried lying—that's not unusual. "He was there for a dental checkup, why do you ask?"

"He wasn't, Caleb. He wasn't on the list of patients. So why was he there? Do you know?"

I could almost see the gears turning in his brain. He was obviously asking himself: should I keep lying and say I didn't know? But rationality set in. That happens sometimes. Rarely; but it happens. Maybe it was because he realized he was talking to a lawyer. The truth was, he said, that Stanley was there on business. What kind of business, I asked? Business... involving the estate of Morris Sylvester. I had no need of probing further. Stanley must have realized that Caleb was taking money from the estate; and he had come to do something about it, or try to.

This cleared something up... but did it shed any light on Maggie's death?

"This place is seriously awful," he said, pushing his plate away. I had to agree. We decided to go elsewhere, for dessert. "I need a dessert," he said. I completely agreed. We found a little shop that sold "designer ice cream," whatever that was supposed to mean. It had a whole list of exotic flavors. Caleb chose vanilla. I chose chocolate. We rejected "tomato peach" and "raspberry cream."

The designer ice cream was extremely good, I have to admit. Not good for a diet, but good for the soul. It seemed to loosen Caleb up: he told me how upset he was by all the rumors that were flying about. "I know," I said. "Take this blackmail business."

But Caleb said, somewhat surprisingly, "Well, it's not entirely wrong... Of course, the idea that Maggie was blackmailing me, that's completely ridiculous. Anybody that knew Maggie.... No, of course it wasn't Maggie. Maggie would never do such a thing. But there was black-mail. From somebody else."

"Who, Caleb?"

"It's funny. I don't really know. I used to get these letters, demanding money. I never paid the money. I just tore the letters up."

"But, Caleb, there must have been something in those letters, you know, some sort of accusation, people don't just ask for money. What were they blackmailing you about?"

"They said they'd tell my wife. About my affair. With Charlotte. Sandra doesn't know. Frank: I'm flesh and blood.... You don't condemn me, do you?"

"Of course not, Caleb. This is the twenty-first century. Queen Victoria's been dead a long time."

I tried to sound broad-minded. And I think I am pretty broad-minded. Though not about myself; Celia would tear me limb from limb if I tried anything.

He went on: "These letters were very crude. Almost illiterate. I have no idea who sent them. I told you, I just tore them up. I talked to Charlotte about it. She wanted to see one of the letters. I showed them to her. She seemed very upset, which is only natural. She told me not to pay any attention to them. She said, call their bluff. Just tear them up, burn them, whatever. She said, be firm. Don't give in."

"And what happened."

"The letters stopped. For a while anyway."

"And you have no idea who wrote them? Be honest, Caleb. You really don't have a clue.?"

"Well, I was wondering.... Maybe Monty Jr. The guy who's suing me. That was my first idea. But the letters, they just didn't seem... well, they were—how can I put it— like somebody really uneducated wrote them.... Unless that was a trick, trying to seem that way, you know, misspelling words. But why would Monty Getz, Jr. care about Charlotte and me? How would he even know about it? I say 'he' but of course I don't know if it was a man or a woman or what."

"And the letters stopped coming?"

"For now. Charlotte said, stop worrying. She's so sensible. Anyway: I don't think Monty Jr. wrote those letters. But I think he's the real Hendrik Borromeo. Monty, that's a nickname. His real name was Montague. Remember Shakespeare, Romeo and Juliet? Well, one of the families was Montague; and here we've got Hendrik Borromeo, think about the Romeo part, you see what I'm driving at."

"And he was coming here to kill you, or threaten you?"

"I think that's what he was going to do. But he didn't get a chance. Maggie was in the way. Somehow he got her out of the building, so I'd be practically alone. Of course I wasn't alone. But... look: this is all very puzzling. Anyway, she came back, sooner than expected. And there was Maggie, and she confronted him. I used to tell her my troubles, she knew all about everything. I think she realized who he was... and she tried to protect me. I was in the back of the place, I couldn't see the reception area, I think she resisted and he killed her...."

It was a possibility. But something about it just didn't make sense to me. As I walked back to the office, I turned things over and over in my mind. Caleb Colegrove had confided in Maggie. He told her secrets. Other people told her secrets, too. And she apparently kept those secrets. One of those secrets was surely the cause of her death.

To me, Caleb Colegrove was an enigma. I couldn't figure him out. I wanted to trust him, but I really had no reason to. He had told me lie after lie. Was he telling me the truth about Charlotte? About her dead child? Was he unaware that she had a living child? Something about the story seemed contrived. But contrived by which one? If I had to guess, I would bet that Charlotte was telling the truth. Or at least some of the truth. What I didn't know, was whether she had told lies, not to me, but to Caleb. Kept her child a secret. But if so, why? Was it because she wanted to go with him to Australia, wanted to start a new life, even have a baby, and her secret offspring would be in the way? I wish I knew.

26

After dinner that evening, Celia disappeared into the room we use as a kind of study, to work on some papers or whatever it was she did for her school. I started reading a novel—a new novel, which Celia's book club was going to discuss, and which Celia insisted I had to read. It was also a new book club; the old one had been broken up by a nasty incident.... I've written that story elsewhere. Anyway, this novel was the latest rage. It was the story of a Korean orphan adopted by a movie star, a woman who ends up having a sexual relationship with the orphan's uncle, who comes to the country, ostensibly on business, but in reality he is an agent of Kim Jung Un, the North Korean dictator. And, oh yes, the uncle is a cross-dresser, who arrives for his liaisons in high heels and lipstick.

I was on page 48, and had had quite enough. The *New York Times* called the book "luminous, gripping... a tale with such deep psychological resonance... that you can't put it down." I had no trouble putting it down, and releasing my grip on the novel. I began thinking, instead, about our local mystery. I tried to tote up all the various theories: why on earth was poor Maggie killed?

My favorite suspect was Dr. Dobbs, possibly because I disliked him. He claimed he wasn't there that morning, but of course he had a key. He could have come in through a back door; after he killed Maggie, he could just disappear the way he had come. Motive? I couldn't think of any, except for the slim chance it was a political hate crime. Dobbs was a right-wing fanatic, who believed people like Maggie were parasites. Does that mean they had no right to live? I realize a crime of this sort could only be committed by a real psychopath. Was Dobbs one of the very few dental psychopaths? I rather doubted it.

Anyway, if Dobbs came in and left, wouldn't Caleb see him? Or Estelle? The office was not that large. I realize that, because of the L-shaped layout, Caleb and Estelle, who were in the back, would see nothing that went on in the reception area. But they would see everything in the back area. Unless Dobbs came in the front door....

My next theory had to do with Xyloquex, this mystery company. Maybe it's a company that does private investigations; maybe it was investigating Dr. Colegrove, something to do with the malpractice case.... That man Brown was an odious character, and just as much of a right-wing lunatic as Dobbs. He reminded me of some sort of Nazi concentration camp guard. But he was much too young for that. I could picture him killing Maggie, but why? On the other hand, she seemed to visit Xyloquex, for some unknown reason. Was there a connection there?

Then there was Dr. Colegrove himself. He had no motive, though, or did he? He claimed to be fond of Maggie. Maggie's daughter corroborated that. Still, Caleb had skeletons in his closet. There was the malpractice case, and Maggie's claim that she knew something about a killing. That just had to be Caleb. She either meant that he had killed his patient, Getz, or perhaps he killed Morris Sylvester. There didn't seem to be a motive for killing Getz, unless it was sheer sadism... but he had a really strong motive for killing the old dentist. He thought he would inherit millions, and Caleb, we know, needed money. And he had never mentioned the codicil to me, with anger or disappointment or indeed with candor; the codicil that cut him out.

Were there other suspects? Chloe? No relative of Celia's could possibly be a killer. Estelle? Charlotte? I hardly knew Estelle. Charlotte did seem a bit more likely. She too made strange trips to Xyloquex. Caleb said Charlotte needed money, too.

All this gave me a terrific headache. I picked up the novel again, but simply couldn't face it. I took a Tylenol and went to bed.

27

I woke up feeling refreshed after a good night's sleep—which is not always the case. I often sleep badly, and wake up feeling anything but refreshed. This morning was different. I'm not sure why. One small thing: somehow, the brain continues to work while we're asleep. I'm convinced of that. For one thing, it churns out ridiculous dreams. But underneath, there's something serious going on. The point is this: in the morning, drinking my coffee and buttering my toast, I had the feeling that I was making progress. Hercule Poirot was not the only one with "little gray cells." All of us have a supply.

Not that I had a solution to the mystery. But I felt I understood the cast of characters... that a lot of things were falling in place, and what remained was to put the pieces together.

And of course, I was not alone. I had Zelda. I liked Zelda. She was off-beat in an innocent, charming way.

I realize that Zelda was at least marginally a suspect. In a mystery novel, she might very well turn out to be the killer. She would confess at the end. Motive? "I was writing a new book. I'm into mysteries, Frank. In this book, somebody gets killed in a particular way, and I wanted to see how the blood would actually spatter. That's why I killed Maggie. It was a huge success. Would you like to read my manuscript?"

In mysteries, the most unlikely person turns out to be the killer. Somebody like Zelda. Or Milo. But in real life....

I was musing about these things, in my office, when I actually got a call from Zelda.

"Frank," she said, "I think I have some new material. I'm dying to share it with you. Provided, of course, you'll share what you have with me."

"Zelda," I said, "you're bound to be disappointed. I'd be happy to hear what you have to say, but I'm afraid I can't give you anything much in return...."

"I found out all sorts of things about Maggie. I've been looking into her life history. It's so interesting! I'd love to be a detective, even an amateur like you, Frank. Did you know Maggie had a lover?"

"A lover? At her age?"

"Frank, don't be prehistoric. My own mother, she's 80, lives in this place, Assisted Living they call it... she can't even dress herself, and she has a boyfriend. I think they drool together, or whatever they do. That's neither here nor there. Anyway, Maggie's lover, that was twenty-five years ago. I think he's dead or something."

"Then why did you bring it up, Zelda?

"Just to say that she had a story. A history. Like everybody. She was complicated, you know? You see an old lady, you think, 'old lady.' That's it. Nothing else. I said to Milo, we were walking in the park, there's this old lady, white hair, pushing a walker, she's got osteoporosis so bad she's practically doubled over. Milo, the sweety, he says something sympathetic, and I said, darling, for all you know, she was a raging sex queen in her day. That could have been Maggie. A sex queen."

"I don't see the connection," I said.

"Frank, I don't see it either. Only, that Maggie's not just an old lady. Or was. She was definitely up to something, that's for sure. She was having secret meetings, with somebody. I found that out. She'd go out of the office, she'd say, I'll be back in half an hour. Very mysterious. And where was she going? She was going over to Xyloquex."

"Xyloquex? What did she have to do with them?"

"I don't know yet. I have a feeling, she might have some sort of connection with the Nazi who runs the place, Werner whatever."

"He's Swiss, Zelda."

"Same difference. Of course, I think it also had something to do with Dr. Colegrove. She was very fond of him, very protective. She felt grateful to him, I guess for the job.... What he felt about her, I'm not sure. I think it was mutual. But I'm not telling you the real news. I'm finding out so many things. And now, I'm pretty sure I know who killed poor Maggie."

"You do? Who was it, Zelda?"

"Estelle."

"You can't be serious."

"I'm extremely serious. I'm using logic. Logic isn't usually what I'm known for, but in this case, it's terrifically useful. I told all this to Milo, I laid it out for him, and he said, sugarplum, you're fantastic. That's the word he used: fantastic. He saw that I had gotten to the bottom of this thing. He's writing a new piece, he's going to call it Z for Zelda, and it's mostly for six xylophones... I know, xylophone starts with an x, but it's pronounced like a z. Same as the Xyloquex corporation. I thought he should call it, Zelda and the Xyloquex, but he reminded me about the copyright issue, and I realized, those people might sue, copyright or whatever, they're vicious. Anyway, he didn't use that name, just Z for Zelda. Or should he call it Zelda and the Xylophone?"

I interrupted the ocean of words: "Please, Zelda, I haven't got all day. Why are you trying to pin this on poor Estelle?"

"Poor my eye. First of all, here's the logic. Was this an inside or an outside job? Inside, because the door was locked. OK: that means either Caleb Colegrove or Estelle. Nobody else was there."

"Nobody that we know of."

She ignored this. "I'm ruling out Colegrove. If you do that, that leaves only one person: Estelle."

"Estelle? It doesn't make sense. I don't know her hardly at all, but still. She's a young dental assistant. Why should she do such a thing?"

"I'm working on that. Maybe it was the money. You know about the money. There was money there. Maggie had the money...."

I did know about the money. I wasn't sure how much Zelda knew. I think I probably knew more than she did, about the money, where it came from. But where had the money been? Did Maggie really stash $25,000 in the office? I doubted it.

I didn't think of Estelle as a likely thief, in any event, let alone a murderess.

"I have a witness, too," Zelda said. "Who saw her coming in the back door. It was the lady from the coffee shop, the one with all the hairspray and the blue fingernail polish, you know who I mean. Felicity."

"The back door? I don't get it. We know Estelle was there that morning, so why do we care if she came in the front door or the back door? And when was this, anyway?"

"She doesn't remember. It was either when she came to work, the hairspray lady, or when she was on a break. She just doesn't remember. It wasn't a big deal to her, at the time. I love her looks, by the way. I'm putting her in my next novel. I'm going to call her Thelma."

"Zelda, I just don't buy this," I said. "And why do you eliminate Colegrove? Under your reasoning, he's the most likely person, I mean, the one who was, well, responsible for this thing."

"He was too fond of Maggie. And Milo says, he didn't do it. Milo has hunches. He's always right. He said to me, Zelda, this man is a dentist. I know him. He's responsible for all of my fillings; you can tell a lot about a man from the way he drills your teeth. That's what Milo said."

I tried to suggest, as gently as I could, that these hunches were hardly evidence of anything. But I didn't want to press the point. After all, I went by my own hunches much of the time. On the other hand, I didn't want to rule out Caleb as a suspect. He seemed to have no motive, granted. On the other hand, this was a man who was taking money illegally from an estate, and who was carrying on an affair with one of his dental assistants. These things are not evidence, either; but they certainly suggest, first, that Caleb was capable of lawless acts, and second, that he was in some ways one fairly desperate dentist.

I started thinking more about Estelle, though. Did I really know her? Charlotte was my dental assistant. I never used Estelle. Estelle was much younger than Charlotte, she was about Chloe's age. And she seemed like... a dental assistant. A young woman who went through whatever training you need to get to be a dental assistant.

It's the same old story, though. All we see is the role. A dental assistant. But Estelle was a human being, with passions and problems and all the rest of it. Maybe she had money problems? I called up Chloe, who I thought might know more about Estelle. "Tell me about Estelle," I said.

"What about her?"

"Just anything. General. What kind of a person she is."

"I don't know her that well. She's been with Dr. Colegrove for a year or two."

"Married, single, boyfriend?"

"She's got a boyfriend. His name is Josh. I don't like him, skinny little guy, with a rat-face, and tattoos all over everything you can see, and god knows what else. I don't know what he does. For all I know, he's a drug pusher... he looks the type."

Not having any personal acquaintance with drug

pushers, and never having laid eyes on Josh, I had nothing to say on this subject. "Could she have... money problems? I mean, Estelle?"

"She told me once, Josh needed money... who knows why. Bail, maybe. He looks like a hoodlum. Maybe he's one of these gang people. Why she sticks with him, I have no idea."

"Do they live together?"

"I have no idea, Frank. I don't know much about her personal life. I think she lives with her mother, in San Carlos. She commutes. That's about all I know."

Chloe had nothing more to contribute about Estelle. Or this Josh. But this did add a new wrinkle. Could Zelda be right? Maybe Estelle tried to get the money from Maggie. Or maybe she opened the door for this Josh person, and he came in and did it. I had half a mind to call the police, and tell them to look into the situation, find out who this Josh person was and investigate him.

I was very excited—I felt tingly all over. I realized that this whole business, the murder, poor Maggie's death, had been really preying on my mind. Who was responsible? Caleb? Or somebody else? Could it be Milo? Was Zelda running around, spinning theories, for no other purpose than to protect Milo from suspicion? Then there was Dr. Dobbs, the right-wing fanatic; and Werner, the mystery man from Xyloquex, sending off drones from his office in suburban San Mateo; or the mysterious Mr. Borromeo, who was either somebody's ex-husband, or ex-boyfriend or who knows what; in any event, he was so shadowy a figure that one wondered if he even existed.

No, Josh was a much better theory. In the first place, I didn't know him. And he seemed so right for the job! Not a dentist, not a businessman or a musician, but a genuine punk, a young hoodlum, the kind with tattoos all over his body—just the thing for a murderer.

I called Zelda and told her the news about Josh. In retrospect, this was a foolish thing to do; but I did it. I think I was so excited that I had to tell someone. The obvious person to tell, of course, was my own dear wife Celia, but the problem was, Celia was too sensible. She was bound to pour cold water over whatever I reported. "I'll tell her later," I said to myself.

Zelda found my report "interesting. A new angle, Frank." She didn't sound totally convinced. "Zelda," I said, "I think we're making progress. Remember, this was basically your idea. About Estelle. And Estelle leads us to Josh. He's the perfect suspect. He probably has a prison record, juvenile hall, that sort of thing. She says he's got tattoos all over, maybe it's a gang thing."

"I have a tattoo, Frank," she said. "On my butt. And so does Milo. We have matching tattoos."

I refrained from asking her what kind of tattoo. "Well, you know what I mean, Zelda," I said. "There are tattoos and tattoos. Gangs have tattoos. I think I read about that somewhere. Or maybe this guy has skulls and swastikas, who knows. The tattoos are not the point. The point is, he seems like somebody who just might be responsible for a crime like this. Suppose Estelle let him in, to steal stuff. Maggie tried to stop him and he killed her. Look: I'm just following up the lead you gave me. So, Zelda, what do you think?"

I could tell from Zelda's voice that she was excited. She kept saying, "Wow. Maybe this is something. You should go to the police, Frank," she said. "They'll arrest this man."

But here the lawyer in me kicked in. "The police? Isn't that a bit hasty, Zelda? I mean, what do we really know? It's just an idea right now. A hunch. We haven't got a shred of evidence. We aren't ready. I was hoping maybe you could, well, follow up on this."

"Well, I will, Frank. And you're right of course. No police. Not yet. Meanwhile, you've got to talk to Estelle."

"Me, Zelda? On what excuse?"

"Do you need an excuse, Frank?"

"Yes, Zelda, I do."

"Well, if you won't talk to her, Frank, I will. Only I want you to be there."

I protested vigorously. I'm afraid I'm not that good at vigorous protests. And Zelda was a force to be reckoned with. She was going to have it out with Estelle, and I simply had to be there. There had to be an attorney present, she said. Of course, that was nonsense, but there was no stopping Zelda, once she made up her mind. In the end I gave in.

I don't know what excuse Zelda gave the poor woman. I think she told her that this was important, that it had to do with Maggie's death. Zelda was, as I knew by now, quite shameless. She hinted strongly that Maggie might have left Estelle some money, that I was handling the estate, and there were legal details to be ironed out.

Estelle must have wondered who Zelda was, and why she was in the picture at all. If so, she never asked. On a bright California afternoon—of course almost all these afternoons are bright—Zelda appeared in my office, with Estelle in tow.

She was a short, thin, mousy young woman, roughly college age. She had brownish hair, big eyes, and a dimpled chin.

"This is about the estate, isn't it?" she asked. She seemed nervous, and her eyes kept darting around the room, as if looking to see if there was a surveillance camera, which of course there was not.

Zelda barged in immediately. "It's not, Estelle. To be perfectly honest. It has nothing to do with the estate. It's about something else."

"But you told me...."

"I was lying, my dear. Just plain lying. If I told you the truth, you wouldn't have come. And it's important for you to have access to a lawyer."

"A lawyer? Why?"

Zelda leaned over toward the woman. She was a good

foot taller, and she brought her face to within inches of Estelle's nose. "Murder is serious business, Estelle."

Estelle opened her mouth; but no words came out. She just stared at Zelda. She seemed genuinely frightened.

Zelda continued: "Your boyfriend, Josh...."

"Oh God. This is about Josh? What's he done now? I swear, he's trying to do the right thing. Really.... People don't understand him...."

"Did you know the police are suspicious of him?" Zelda asked, in the tone of a grand inquisitor.

"Suspicious? About what?"

Zelda lowered her voice to a hiss: "Maggie...."

"Maggie? What about Maggie?"

"Somebody killed her, Estelle," Zelda said. "Of course you know that. Now Josh...."

"Josh? Maggie? Oh, you can't be serious. What are you trying to say? You can't mean you think he had something to do with this awful thing. Oh God, you can't."

The poor girl was on the verge of tears. She kept knotting her fingers in and out of each other, and her voice trembled. But there was no stopping Zelda. "Oh, can't we? We can. And I think the police are suspicious. Maybe you let him in the door, you opened the door for him, and then he did it. That would make you an accomplice, Estelle. Do you know what that means? You were there, after all. You could have let him in."

Estelle now had a look of sheer terror on her face. She looked like some sort of character in a slasher movie, a young girl face to face with a maniac, who was about to slice and dice her to death. Or was she simply astonished? She turned to me in a panic. "Mr. May," she said, "what is this woman saying? Josh wouldn't kill anybody. He couldn't do a thing like that. Anyway, that morning, the morning she was killed, Josh.... He wasn't there. He couldn't have had anything to do with it, I swear."

Zelda said: "I suppose you think he had an alibi.

Alibis are flimsy, my dear. Where was he, Estelle? What was his alibi?"

Estelle was now sobbing and moaning. "Josh... he couldn't have.... He was in jail. I warned him, he was going to get in trouble again.... He went out drinking with some of his buddies. He was supposed to take me out, but he said he couldn't, I don't know what gets into him—he's got these friends, they're totally no good, totally. They were drinking, playing pool, God knows what. Smoking pot, I think. Oh God. I think there was some kind of fight, in this place where they were, I don't know exactly what happened, he drove off, the car belonged to one of the guys. And they got in some kind of accident, the police picked him up; he's got so many black marks against him, he's been in trouble so much, I'm afraid he'll lose his license, drunk driving. I told his mother, I would get him to stop, stop drinking and driving, but when he's with these guys, there's nothing I can do. Especially one of them, they call him Ernie, he's just plain no good, I don't know what Josh sees in him, but oh God, what's the use. Josh can be sweet, really, but he's weak, he's with this bad crowd.... Anyway they threw him in jail, overnight, and I had to go get him out, in the morning.... His mom couldn't do it, she works, and she's got a heart condition...."

"So he was in jail? Can you prove it?" Zelda's voice was harsh. But of course if Estelle was telling the truth, which she probably was, the proof would be easy, even though, right now, she simply kept on sobbing. The whole Josh theory was vanishing in a puff of smoke.

Zelda must have felt the same way: so much for Josh. But that left Estelle herself. As far as I was concerned, she was also out of the picture. This timid creature was completely incapable of an act of such brutality. Zelda, however, was not giving up so fast.

"What time did you go get him?" she asked.

"I don't remember. Late morning, sometime. I mean, it was all a blur. I got a call from Charlotte, about Maggie being dead, you can imagine how I felt when I picked up the phone. I thought, oh God, what a day, first Josh, then this...."

It took a second for all of this to register with me. What she had said. But then something clicked in my brain. "Estelle," I said, "you had a call from Charlotte? At home?"

"Yes, I was home...."

"But I thought... I thought you were at the office. Didn't you just say, Charlotte called you from the office? Let me get this straight. We thought you were at the office—and Charlotte was home. You seem to suggest the exact opposite. Could you explain this?"

To my surprise, my question produced a hysterical fit of sobbing. I tried to calm her down; I keep a box of tissues on my desk, and I handed her one. "Oh, Mr. May!" she said, between sobs. "What have I done?"

"I don't know. What have you done?"

"I've been lying to you. I wasn't there at all. I mean, I came later on, when Charlotte called me. I was home. She called. She told me Maggie was dead. She said, I had to come to the office. She said, it was a matter of life and death. I said, why, what's the reason? She wouldn't say. I don't live far away, I live in San Carlos, with my mom... I was at home, I got up early, because, well, I was worried about Josh. Anyway, I came right down, and they let me in through the back door. And there was the doctor, you know, Dr. Colegrove, and Charlotte, and they seemed so terribly upset, and they made me swear I would help them. I mean, they said it was about Maggie, that they had nothing to do with it, but they needed my help."

"What kind of help?"

"They said, the police were on the way. They called the police. They found the body and they called the police. And they said, I had to say I was there, and Charlotte wasn't. And I said, oh, I can't do that, it's a lie, and the police... you can't lie to the police I said. They said, I had to do it, they'd explain it sometime, but they begged and pleaded and... I still wouldn't do it. Not at first. But then... oh, I'm so embarrassed and ashamed."

"Ashamed of what, Estelle?"

"What I did. They said, they knew I needed money. They knew about Josh, and all the problems...."

"How did they know that?"

"Oh, I told Charlotte about him, and about things.... I talk too much, Mr. May. I know that now. I told her all sorts of things, and now... well, they offered me money. To tell the lie. And... I took it. They gave me some money, I think it was $200, they said, that's all the cash they had, but they promised a lot more."

"And did they pay more?"

More tears. "Yes. Hundreds of dollars. Later on that is. A week or so. Oh, Mr. May, I didn't want to do it, I didn't want to lie. But they were so insistent... you believe me, don't you? And then I went and got Josh out of jail... that morning... after I talked to the police, and told them the lie. Anyway, I thought, well, I am here right now, so it's not so big a lie, just a bit of a lie about when I got there, and Charlotte was so grateful...."

I'll bet she was. And my little gray cells began churning. What was it Zelda had said—about logic? Estelle was the prime suspect, because she was there. But in fact she wasn't there. Charlotte was there. That meant, by the same logic, that the finger of blame now pointed squarely at Charlotte.

We promised to keep Estelle's secret, at least for the time being. Four tissues later, she was calm enough to go home.

When she left, I turned to Zelda, and said: "Charlotte." Just the one word: Charlotte. But she understood, and nodded her head.

28

After Estelle left, Zelda gave me a broad grin, and said: "Frank, we're finally making real progress."

"We are?"

"Oh, I know, we had some wrong ideas. I mean, I did. Not you. You were right as usual. You never thought Estelle was the one. You're so clever, Frank! You really are a great detective. Anyway, now we know the true state of affairs."

"And what's that, Zelda?"

"It's Charlotte. Or Dr. Colegrove himself. Or the two of them. They're lovers, after all. They must have done it. Maybe they did it together."

"But why? You don't kill people just like that, out of the blue, for no reason. And you yourself said that you ruled out Dr. Colegrove."

"I'm ruling him back in," Zelda said. "I can make mistakes, like everybody else. I'm going to put a dentist into my next book, he's going to be a killer. He seems like a harmless man in a white coat... let me see, is he old or young? I don't know yet. I was going to have him look like Caleb. He's a sadist, he can't help killing people. He puts poison in the drill, then he grinds their teeth and kills them in the chair. Do you think that would work out, Frank? It'll be a new genre for me. No more romance. Violent death, that's the thing."

"Really, Zelda...."

"And maybe he rapes women, or is that too gross? He

kills the women patients, and he rapes them. Maybe that would sell, but I don't know if I could do it, Frank. I have literary principles. That just isn't my thing. I have to think about this. If I call my dentist Caleb, is that too obvious?"

"I wouldn't do that, Zelda."

"Then I won't. I have to talk to Milo about this. He's writing this concerto for dentist and orchestra; maybe he'll want to change it. Oh, I know Milo... he's not going to give up this idea, just because of Caleb Colegrove and my suspicions. No, but maybe he'll change the tone of it. Make it darker. More tubas and trombones. Milo will know what to do."

She was off and running. I won't bore you with the rest of the conversation. She was all for confronting Caleb and Charlotte. I tried to talk her out of it, which was impossible. She brought up the question of going to the police, but this was a nonstarter. We had nothing real to go on. Oh yes, Estelle had lied. Charlotte was there that morning. But this was no evidence, and there was nothing concrete. And above all, no motive. Why would anyone want to kill Maggie? And least of all Charlotte... and Caleb Colegrove, D.D.S.

But I certainly agreed that we were making progress. Particularly in deciding who had lied and who had told the truth. Charlotte and Caleb had lied. But someone else had lied as well. I was trying to reconstruct the chronology in my mind—what had transpired that morning, and when. When had they called Estelle? I had the feeling that something was all wrong with the timeline. Somebody had killed Maggie. As far as we know, nobody was there in the office, except for Caleb and Charlotte. The door mysteriously closed, and then opened. And when it was opened, in came Stanley.

Stanley. Something was wrong here. Something about Stanley's story just didn't ring true to me. Was he part of whatever plot there was here? Some sort of cover-up?

As luck would have it, I had a meeting with Stanley a day or so later. We were on opposite sides of a family quarrel, a dispute over an inheritance. This had turned quite nasty, which is, alas, far from rare. Stanley represented the young second wife of an old man, Walker Wheelwright, who had disinherited his children by his first marriage, all five of them. He left everything to the new wife. They had been married less than a year. Both Stanley and I wanted to settle the case, which was the sensible thing to do, if we could only get the parties to stop spitting venom at each other and vowing to fight the thing to the death.

It was a delicate business, because Stanley and I were officially enemies in this case, although we both understood what had to be done, which the parties certainly did not. At any rate, when we left Stanley's office, he and I had coffee together in downtown Palo Alto. And after talking over the Wheelwright case, I felt bold enough to confront Stanley. "Can I switch the subject, Stanley?" I said.

"Please! I'm sick of these neurotic Wheelwrights. What's on your mind?"

"Stanley, don't take offense. But I think you've been lying to me."

"Me? Lie? OK, I won't say that I never told a lie to a client or an attorney, in my forty years of practice.... But, Frank, you think I lied to you? What on earth about?"

"This business with Caleb Colegrove. The receptionist, Maggie. The story you told us. The door is locked, then the door is open, you find a body, your fly is open, all of that: frankly, Stanley, I think you fed me, and everybody else, a large load of bullshit."

He had a sly look on his face. I couldn't read him. "Lie to you, Frank? Now why would I do that? You don't think my fly was really open?"

"Maybe it was, maybe it wasn't, Stanley. I think it was a nice touch, a nice way to gussy up a story. I think you're part of a cover-up. Something fishy was going on in that office."

"Hmm," he said, "something fishy. Maybe traffic in gold? Fillings made out of plastic, colored to look like gold? Is that what was going on? Or—wait—maybe you think Caleb was running a Ponzi scheme in his spare time."

"Be serious, Stanley," I said. "This is about murder. Murder is a serious business. Poor Maggie is dead...."

"You think I killed her? Listen, if I felt like killing somebody, I'd kill one of your clients, this guy George Wheelwright, the ringleader, the one who's driving my client crazy. I'd kill him in a heartbeat, if I thought I could get away with it. But Maggie, no."

"Don't make jokes, Stanley. Maggie knew a secret that maybe cost her her life. She knew that Caleb had killed somebody. I think you knew that too."

"Really. And who was Caleb supposed to kill?"

"Actually, Stanley, I'm not sure. Either this patient of his, Getz... or maybe Morris Sylvester. One of the two."

Stanley smiled. He had been eating a big slice of carrot cake. He took the last forkful and shoveled it into his mouth. The waiter came and handed him the bill. Stanley reached into his wallet, took out some money, put it down on the table, on top of the check. Then he put down the fork and got up. He looked me straight in the eye, and said: "You know what, Frank? You've got this reputation, great detective, great amateur detective, everybody says that, they say that Frank denies it, but really he's got a knack. Well, in fact, Frank, you're right and they're wrong. You're not a great detective. You're nothing. That reputation is based on hot air. You couldn't solve your way out of a paper bag. And you just proved it, once again."

And with that he left the restaurant.

I sat there, in a bit of a daze.

29

I was hurt and angry. Stanley's words kept ringing in my brain. They stung like the sting of a wasp. I spent a lot of time at home (and, frankly, also at the office) mulling and chewing and trying to connect the dots. What did Stanley mean by his mean, sarcastic remarks? I guess the point was that I was way off base. But in what regard?

Charlotte was still the number one suspect, as far as I could see. Of course, we had nothing concrete, nothing we could go to the police with. Which is just as well. And yet—should I talk to Charlotte? It was likely, I suppose, that Estelle had told her everything about our conversation.

For a couple of days, though, I basically did nothing. Not literally, of course: I do have a profession, and I was hard at work. But on the Maggie affair, this was a dormant period. A period of thinking and worrying.

I had to talk to somebody, and who better than my dear wife, Celia? I brought her completely up to date. I got the usual (good) advice: keep out of it. This was not a surprise. She was knitting a sweater for a colleague, who had just had a baby at the age of 44. I could tell by the way the needles moved that Celia was annoyed with me. "Promise you'll stop what you're doing," she said.

"I'm not doing anything. Not now. I just talked to some people. I promised Maggie's daughter."

"You promised her, but you won't promise me?"

I had no answer. Still, I never did make the promise—

to Celia, that is. Celia would have insisted, I'm sure of that. But just then the phone rang. It was her friend Myrna, the English teacher with the new baby, and Celia got caught up in some complex affair involving something going on at the school, or some rich item of gossip. I never found out what, but it was engrossing enough to allow me to escape and go to bed.

The next day, Estelle called me on the phone. Between sobs, she told me how sorry she was about everything, and she went on and on about how terrible she felt, she doesn't know what got into her, and so on and so forth. And things were going badly with Josh, she was going to have to break up with him, but she loved him so, and what was she to do? I had very little interest in her love life, but she confirmed that she had confessed all to Charlotte—that is, she told Charlotte that she had spoken to me "and also to that other women, the tall one with the long nose," and that we knew her secret and she was so ashamed of herself. And she was going to go to the police and tell them she had lied. She just had to do this. She couldn't sleep, and she was losing weight and she couldn't lose weight, she was too thin as it was. And her mother told her, she had to tell the truth; her mother knew the whole story now, and her mother was very angry with her. She didn't get along with her mother anyway, and her mother said, she had to get rid of that bum, she called Josh a bum and they ended up screaming at each other, literally screaming, and she had a terrific headache.

I said a few comforting platitudes.

"I'm not going to do it right away, though," she said. "The police, I mean. But, Mr. May, would you talk to Charlotte, please? Ask her what this is all about. I just don't have the nerve. You don't think she killed Maggie, do you?"

"I honestly don't know what to think," I said.

I suspected that any conversation with Charlotte would be awfully unpleasant. Or would end up in silence. But I felt it had to be done. Was it possible that we were nearing the end of the road? Charlotte and Caleb: they had to be part of the answer. They had to be deeply involved. I could hear Celia, my inner voice, telling me to "be sensible, for once. Don't rush into something that doesn't concern you."

Why was it my affair? I could always choose another dentist. In fact, Celia had. For some reason, she never liked Caleb Colegrove. She had abandoned him years before, for a woman dentist, Dr. Hilary Smuts. I could do the same.

But Estelle was still on the phone, and still on my conscience. She begged me to go to Charlotte and find out why they had asked her to come to the office. "Am I some sort of accomplice? I just couldn't stand that, Mr. May. Really. If you could only help me...."

"Estelle," I said, "are you asking me to tell Charlotte we think she killed somebody? That's not easy to do."

"Tell her you're my lawyer—aren't you my lawyer, Mr. May? And that your client wishes to go to the police, and did she have anything to say...."

I could hear the quiver in her voice. The poor girl was crying. And I am weak. A woman's tears always get to me. Celia doesn't cry very much. Maybe that's why we're a successful couple. Crying clients—that's another story.

In the end, I gave my promise. I thought: I can do this. I can be very judicious, very lawyerly. And what would happen to me? Charlotte was certainly not going to kill me. Dental assistants don't do things like that. It was a mantra I repeated constantly to myself.

I called Zelda later, on her cellphone. She sounded breathless, and I heard vague noises in the background. "Where are you, Zelda?" I asked.

"I'm on a treadmill, Frank. At my health club. I'll call you back when I finish," Zelda said.

When she called, fresh no doubt from a successful war on calories, I explained to her what had gone on, my phone conversation with Estelle. And she said, with a real note of triumph in her voice, "We did it, Frank."

"Did what?"

"Solved the case. It was Charlotte. She did it. She did it for the money. Or maybe she was blackmailing him, blackmailing Caleb."

"Zelda, she's in love with him. Why would she blackmail him?"

"Love? What's love? Who knows. There could be all sorts of reasons. I was thinking about something I could put in another book, or maybe a novella. Frank, you wouldn't believe how much this business has inspired me. I have all these ideas running around in my head. I almost fell off the treadmill, they were so exciting."

"Ideas?"

"Book ideas. I wish I could write them much faster! Anyway: there's this dentist. Real proper type, on the outside. He lives in Atherton, in a mansion. A house with ten bathrooms. He's the most successful dentist in the whole Bay Area. But that's because he sold his soul to the devil, and the devil made sure he became filthy rich. He practices satanic rituals, right in his office, after he drugs his patients. Maybe when they wake up, they don't even realize what's happened. Or maybe he hypnotizes them and makes them sign over all their money. I haven't worked out the details yet. But it's promising."

Zelda's new book held no interest for me. I was wondering: had we really solved the case? For my part, I wasn't quite so sure. I was suspicious of Charlotte: she had been lying to us; but the reasons were obscure. And, if I had to pick a prime suspect, my own choice would be Caleb Colegrove. In both cases, we were still flailing about for a motive.

30

The next day, in the late morning, I had a gap in my appointment schedule. I resisted the almost overwhelming urge to put off taking the next logical step in this business. But I screwed up my courage and nonchalantly walked across the street, to Dr. Colegrove's office. A new girl, a stranger to me, was sitting at the reception desk. Chloe was next to her. I asked her if I could speak to Charlotte.

She was busy, I was told, so I sat down in the small reception area, and picked up a magazine. It was Sunset, and it had an article on how to make pickled artichokes, which I skipped; the next article told the reader how to get the most out of a touristic visit to Fresno. I was about to read this article, wondering what it might possibly have to say, since Fresno had always struck me as close to absolute zero from the touristic standpoint. I never got the chance, because Charlotte appeared and said hello.

"Good to see you, Frank," she said. "Are you here for a checkup?"

"Not exactly," I said.

"Are you having a problem? Doctor is tied up all morning, but if it's an emergency...."

"Oh, no, nothing like that," I said.

"Are you flossing, Frank? I warned you about your gums, last time, at least I think I did. I tell all my patients, floss, floss, floss. Most of them do it. It's important. I know you're stubborn, Frank... but I didn't think you'd be back so soon. Oh: I forgot. You were going to come in for your regular visit..." She didn't have to add why that visit was aborted. We both remembered, all too well.

"Charlotte," I said, "Can I speak to you in private? This isn't about flossing or anything to do with my teeth. It's about Maggie.

"Maggie? What about her?" Was that a look of panic on her face?

"This isn't the place to have this conversation, Charlotte...."

She led me into the back of the suite, into a room which was not in use at the moment. I wondered if Dr. Dobbs was at work somewhere else, or Dr. Colegrove, or both. I heard the sound of a high-speed drill in another office.

I asked Charlotte to close the door.

"What's this about, Frank?"

"I don't know how to say this, Charlotte."

"Say what?"

"I've been talking to Estelle," I said.

"To Estelle? What on earth about?"

She acted as if this was a big surprise, but I knew she must be faking. She knew what Estelle had told us. I plunged boldly ahead, giving my own version of the story. It wasn't exactly gospel truth, but it was close enough.

"Estelle came to me for legal advice," I said, "and of course whatever she said to me was said in confidence. But I had to tell her, she was potentially in a lot of trouble. Lying to the police is not a trivial matter."

Charlotte stared at me. I expected her to say something defensive; instead, she was very quiet.

"I talked it over with her. It's her decision, of course. I felt, personally, that she has to go to the police. And I think she will. She's made up her mind. This thing is preying on her mind. But she asked me to talk to you first, before she did anything. She asked me to find out what you have to say."

Still silence.

"The point is," I said, "that she lied when she said she was here that morning. The morning that Maggie died. She wasn't here at all. Not until later. You called her and told her she had to come. You and Caleb, I guess. When she came, Maggie was already dead. You gave her money, and made her promise to tell the police that she was here when... when Maggie died—and that you, Charlotte, were not in the office at all. Isn't that correct?"

She was as pale as a ghost. Then she said: "Why are you doing this, Frank? What's the point of it?"

"I'm representing my client," I said. "And the point is, Charlotte, I want to give you a chance to explain yourself. Are you going to deny what she said? Are you saying that Estelle is making this whole thing up?"

A short silence. Then she said: "No, Frank, she was telling the truth."

I guess I was having an adrenalin high. Later on, I was amazed that the words could actually come out of my mouth. "Then... what are people supposed to think, Charlotte? I mean, this was pretty strange behavior, no? Asking this girl to lie for you. And why? The police were going to come. A crime had been committed. They were going to investigate, going to try to find out what happened. You knew that there'd be almost nobody in the office, you arranged to get Maggie out of the office somehow, then you locked the door. But she got back in, maybe she had a key, and then, well, you know as well as I do what happened next: she ended up dead, lying on the floor in the bathroom. I think you called Stanley, too.... I think he was lying too, I don't think he just came in, and happened to find the body."

She was pale as a ghost. "What are you driving at, Frank? Are you saying I killed Maggie? Me?"

"Well, if it wasn't you, who else? Caleb? He was here too."

She burst into tears. "Charlotte," I said, "I'm not

going to make anything of this... it's none of my business. I'm only representing Estelle. Was it the money? Was it the cash, was there cash in the office that day, Dobbs' payment, you know, the $25,000? Did you need it? Was that what this was all about?"

"The money?" she said, seeming to pull herself together. "Is that your idea? But Caleb and I... we were going to go to Australia. Why would I want the money? It was ours.... You're not making sense, Frank. Why would I kill Maggie? Why would Caleb kill Maggie?"

"I know I'm not making sense," I said. "But somebody killed her, and the police are bound to find out. After they hear from Estelle, they'll be terrifically suspicious. Why did this woman lie? What was happening here, locked doors, and all that stuff? You could kiss your Australia plans goodbye. You and Caleb."

"That's not very nice of you, Frank," she said. "I don't like your tone."

"Well, what tone do you expect, Charlotte? Something really fishy is going on here, that's clear."

Another short silence. Then she said: "Frank, you just don't understand."

"I guess I don't."

Another pause. Then she said. "I have to talk to Caleb. I'm awfully sorry about Estelle. I shouldn't have put her in this position. Things have been... complicated, Frank. More than you realize. I want you to talk to Caleb and me.... Can you come back later, after the office is closed... say six o'clock?"

I agreed. It was only later that I had a few doubts. In the first place, it meant I would get home late. This is something Celia really hates, and it happens far too often. Then, in the second place, I would be alone, trapped in a dentist's office with two people, one of whom, or both, could be killers. I told myself this fear was ridiculous, but I wasn't quite convinced. I called Celia and told her I'd be late.

"Must you, Frank? For a change, the girls are both home for dinner, and that friend of theirs, she's coming too. You know, the short one with the curly hair, she's got a twin brother, I forget her name. I really wanted you to be around. I thought you'd help me get dinner on the table."

I told her that I had to see Dr. Colegrove and his assistant, at 6:00. I did this not only because it was true, but because I wanted Celia to know where I was and when I would be there, just in case there was any trouble. "What for?" she asked. "Seems like a funny time to see a dentist."

"Honey, it's not about dentistry. It's legal stuff."

"Legal stuff? What does that mean?"

I hate to lie. But I felt trapped. "You know I can't talk to you about my clients' business."

"Honestly, Frank. What's this all about? You tell me lots of things. Then, when it suits your purposes, you clam up entirely."

"I do talk, my dear, about clients; you're right—but within limits, definite limits." So I said what I had to say, and found a graceful way to hang up the phone.

31

I have to admit I had some queasy feelings when I crossed the street and rang the bell at the office door. It was late in the year, and the sun was already sinking. The street lights were on, but the front door was in the shadows. I hated to be there alone with them—a dentist's office is not the most cuddly place even under normal circumstances. There were all those drills and other torture instruments. I had visions of being executed with huge doses of X-rays.

Charlotte opened the door. She was pale and looked extremely nervous. "It's good of you to come, Frank."

She took me into one of the back rooms. Dr. Colegrove was already there. He also looked pale and nervous. She said, "Excuse me for a minute." She went into another room, and I heard her whispering to somebody. I was puzzled. There was somebody else here, in the office, besides the two of them... who could that be?

Charlotte came back. "Would you like some coffee, Frank? Or tea?" I said no.

There was an awkward silence. Then Caleb spoke. "Frank, I want you to be honest with us. We're going to be honest with you. You think I killed Maggie, don't you?"

I hemmed and hawed. "Not really, Caleb... I mean, how would I know? There are some things that... well, that seem suspicious."

"You really think I'm capable of killing somebody?"

Did I dare tell him what I thought? I guess I did: I came right out and said it: "Well, Maggie thought so."

"Maggie?" He seemed genuinely astonished. "She thought I killed somebody? You can't be serious, Frank."

"Well," I said. "She didn't name names. But she told somebody that she knew about some sort of killing... and I assumed...."

"You assumed?" he said, raising his voice. "You assumed it was me? But why, Frank?"

"Really, Caleb," I said sheepishly, "I never accused you.... I mean, it was just... Maggie thought.... Anyway, maybe she was referring to that patient, Getz, the one that died, or maybe Morris Sylvester...."

"Morris Sylvester? She thought I killed Morris?"

"She didn't actually say.... I was just thinking.... Don't be angry, Caleb. I mean, I had no idea who she could've had in mind.... And Dr. Sylvester, well, it was supposed to be suicide, but... he had this will, and he named you in it...."

"For God's sake, Frank. What a monster you must think I am! To think I killed Morris Sylvester, my partner. You can't imagine how insane that idea is. My partner. A sweet, harmless old man."

"OK, OK," I said, backing off. "But then.... What did Maggie mean?"

"I'll tell you, since you're so anxious to know. It was Morris himself. He killed his old mother. It was one of those mercy killings. She was old, demented, half-blind, suffering, in constant pain; it was pathetic. He loved her madly, and he just couldn't watch her die a slow, agonizing death. She begged him.... He came to me for advice. Me and Maggie, by the way. We told him, don't do it. Maybe that was wrong. We said, let nature take its course, we sympathized, well, I did, more than Maggie actually. We weren't harsh, no, but Maggie said something about leaving it to God or whatever. But in the end he did it."

"And... killed himself?"

"Absolutely. He was tortured by guilt. That was the

thing, his guilt. He just couldn't take it. Besides, he had been so attached to her, he had no other family, no life really, except my office, and that just wasn't enough. He felt he couldn't go on living."

"And the will...."

"OK, sure, I would have liked the money. He had a lot of money. But I didn't even know that he left it to me. Honest to God, I didn't know. He had nobody else to leave it too, that's all. But after his mother died, the guilt and all that, he decided, no, I need to do something else with my money, I need to make amends. And that's why he left it to charity, part of it, to help poor people, you know, with their teeth—and part of it in his mother's memory, with that flower group, the one his mother had been active in. And that's the honest truth; that's the story. At least the story about Morris."

Charlotte had been quiet the whole time. Then she spoke: "Now, Frank, we have to tell you the rest of it. The part about Maggie."

I said, "If you want to. You don't have to."

She said: "But we do have to. Estelle is going to go to the police. They'll start asking questions. I don't know how you stumbled onto things, but you did."

I nodded, as if in agreement. To be perfectly honest, I had no idea what I'd stumbled onto, if anything. I could see I had been wrong about so many things—Morris Sylvester, for example. But maybe I was right about Caleb and Charlotte.

She said, "There's a lot on my conscience, Frank. Me more than Caleb. Things we don't want to hide any longer. You found out about Estelle. And Stanley. We knew we can't pretend anymore. We'll tell you the whole story, from our own point of view—I don't know what you're thinking, whether you blame us, but anyway.... I'm rambling, I know that. But Frank, we're on the ropes. Maybe you can give us some advice. We're in a terrible situation."

Was this a confession?

"A situation," I said. "Maggie, you mean."

She burst into tears. Caleb put his arm around her. "It's not your fault," he said. "You mustn't feel guilty."

"You tell him," she said.

"'No, you, Charlotte." But she shook her head and sobbed. So he said: "All right."

"I really didn't know what was going on," he said. "That morning. Charlotte was talking to me, there was something funny going on, nobody seemed to be in the office. She had actually cancelled some people, and she was talking and talking—stalling, it seemed to me. Then we heard a noise. Somebody yelled. I wanted to go see what it was, Charlotte said, don't go, but of course I went, and what did I see: I saw this guy, this young guy... and he was babbling something, I couldn't make out what it was. Maggie was lying there, and Charlotte put her arm around the guy. I said, what's happening, what is this nitwit doing here. And she said: he's my son."

I thought: her son? Who was that? Was it that Josh person, Estelle's boyfriend? But then he came in, from the other room, It wasn't Josh. It was Judd. His hair was rumpled, he was wearing a torn T-shirt, and he looked truly awful.

"This is your son?" I asked, incredulous.

"Yes, yes, he is," she said, in between sobs. "It's a long story. I was very young, and I wasn't married.... I gave him up for adoption.... My family talked me into it," she said. "But then, a year or so ago, I traced him and I found him. I felt so guilty about giving him up; I don't think he was raised right. Maggie was so wonderful, she helped me out. If I had known how things would work out, oh God!" she said, and burst into violent tears.

Judd just stood there; with a blank stare on his face. She buried her face in her hands. Then she said. "I was so stupid! I didn't dare tell Caleb about it. Here finally I had a chance in life, I had somebody who loved me, and, yes, I love him, and I was so afraid that, if he knew about Judd.... I got him this job, at that company, and I went there to see him from time to time, or Maggie went, with messages, and I gave him money...."

I was trying to take it all in. "What are you saying, Charlotte? What happened? Was it... Judd? I mean... Maggie...."

She was crying hysterically now, and nodding her head.

"Charlotte," Caleb said, "you should have had more faith in me. This wouldn't have happened. This mess we're in." He turned to me. "I didn't know what was going on. When we came out from the back, and there was Judd, and Maggie lying on the floor. I could see that she was dead, I took her pulse. And Judd, he was crying, saying over and over again, it was an accident, and Charlotte was screaming. And she said, Caleb, this is my son. You can imagine my shock. Maggie, dead on the floor, blood all over the place, and Charlotte telling me, this jerk was her son. He was wailing, and talking about accident accident accident. And I realized, we had to do something. And Charlotte pleaded with me, she said, Caleb, you have to help us, he didn't mean any harm, she begged me and begged me, and... I did what she wanted."

"But what happened?" I asked. "Why did he... do what he did? What happened to poor Maggie?"

"Tell him, Judd," Charlotte said.

The kid sat down in a chair, he was fidgeting, crying, and the words came out in a rush. "I wanted the money," he said. "It was the money. I knew that other lady, she wasn't there, and I thought, hey, maybe this is the time. I knew about the money. My mom told me about the money, she told me about Australia, you know, and how Dobbs was giving them money, cash. She said, maybe I'd come with them, she'd tell him about me, she wouldn't keep it secret anymore, and we could start over, in Australia, shit, it sounded good to me. I didn't know Maggie had it in a bank account. I thought she had a pile of cash and she was hiding it in the office.... I mean, I guess I was stupid.... Anyway, I heard that these dentists, too, they have stuff, drugs, stuff you can sell, man I needed money. I had a fight with the people that raised me, I never got along with them, I hated them, especially the dad, he was a real strict bastard, and I ran away from them. I got this girl in trouble, high school girl, she was a little tramp, I thought she was 18, it was at this party.... Never mind.... She wants to get rid of the kid. It takes money, and my mom, this mom here, the new mom, whatever you want to call her, she wouldn't give me the money. I wanted to buy stuff, too. I thought they owed it to me...."

"He's not bad," Charlotte said, in a shrill voice. "He didn't mean any harm. It's not his fault. I'm the one, it's my fault. I should have given him the money."

Something popped into my head. "He wrote those letters. The blackmail letters to Caleb."

"Oh, God," she said. "Yes. When Caleb showed me those letters, I knew it was Judd. I told him, he had to stop. I said I would get him money, somehow; but I didn't. And I guess I shouldn't have told him about the money, the money from Dobbs... but I had to, I mean, when I was telling him about Australia, and the plans to go to Australia.... oh God, I should have kept my mouth shut, but I wanted to give him a life. I wanted to give myself a life...."

"I wanted to go to Australia," he said, "I heard stuff about Australia. She said she'd take me along, like I said. And I want to get out of this bullshit nothing job, working for those Nazis over there. I want a real job, I want to fix computers, cars, radios, whatever, learn how to do this stuff. Maggie, she used to come talk to me, where I worked. I said, my mom, you know? She's ashamed of me, she gave me away when I a kid, don't think that doesn't mean something to me. She never wanted me. Then she comes back into my life, she gives me this big 'I'm your real mother' shit.... Look, I don't blame her. She got her hooks on this fancy dentist, real professional, a guy with money.... I figured, she doesn't really want me around...."

"Oh God, no, Judd!" she said. "I love you." Dr. Cole-grove was silent, tight-lipped.

Judd went on: "She told me about the money, it was when we talked about Australia. That's when I thought, I'll make the doctor pay, that's what I'll do. So I wrote those letters, but she told me I had to stop, and he wasn't going to pay anyway. The money: I thought, it's cash, and Maggie has it, she keeps it in the office, I just wanted to look around. I called Maggie on my cellphone, I said come on out, I have to talk to you, hey, it's important, it's a matter of life and death. She said I can't leave the office empty I said yes you can, it's just for a short time. I wanted to get her out of the way. Then I went back in and I hid in the restroom, and the idea was, mom would talk to the guy, the dentist. She didn't want to do it...."

"Oh why did I ever say yes!" Charlotte said, in a kind of moan.

"I talked her into it," he said, "I said, you got to do this for me, stall him out, talk about something, some dental shit, or else don't come in at all, but she did come in. She said, are you going to steal something? I said, look, you got to do this, and you're my mom, and I said if she didn't I'd rob somebody else...."

She said: "I was at my wit's end. I didn't know what to do. But then I did what he asked me. I'm weak...."

He said, "Anyway, I was looking for the money, and just then, Maggie came back in... I guess I was stupid. She said, what are you doing here, and I said none of your business. I had a knife in my hand, and she saw it. She was about to scream, so I covered her mouth, she started to try to yell, we sort of struggled, and she fell and I lost it, God help me, I banged her head. I had to stop her from screaming and all that... and I don't know, there was blood all over the place. I didn't mean to hurt her, I swear I didn't. And then I thought, oh shit, now I'm really in trouble. And I dragged her into the toilet, the stall, and I dumped her there."

Caleb turned to me and said, "We came back here, me and Charlotte; and we found her, and I said, oh my God, she's dead. And this guy was there, Judd, and Charlotte blurted out that he was her son, and he said, it was an accident, please believe me. Then Charlotte said, this will ruin his life, Caleb, please, you've got to give him a chance, he says it was an accident and it must have been. I should have done nothing, but... you know, it was a crisis, we had to act fast. We told him to get the hell out of there, and he did, and I said to Charlotte, this is insane, but she kept begging me to help. So we locked the door and cleaned up the blood. I said to Charlotte, OK, now, we have to call the police, but she wouldn't let me."

She said, "I knew it was wrong, but I was desperate. We were taking a big chance. I said, I would figure something out. We called Estelle, made her come down, we cleaned up the rest of the blood, and then we let Stanley in the front door."

He said: "We were taking a huge risk. Gigantic. We figured, maybe nobody would use the bathroom, till we could get rid of the body. We were going to cancel all the rest of the appointments, call people, tell them I was sick or make some excuse. We took her shoes off. We were planning somehow to hustle her body away, wrapped up in something. Charlotte hid the shoes, the simplest way, she just put them on, and put her own shoes in a closet; she was wearing running shoes anyway, well, that doesn't matter. But it all went wrong. Stanley told us, we just couldn't do that, we wouldn't get away with it, and we'd be breaking the law in ten different ways. He said, get Charlotte out of here, that's the right move. Let the police come, and it'll be a big mystery, they'll think somebody broke in. It's your only chance. Just keep your mouths shut, play dumb... look: you didn't do anything, so a few little lies won't matter."

I didn't know what to say. Judd was sitting in a kind of stupor, looking down at his feet, and sobbing. Charlotte was sobbing. It was a kind of chorus of sobs. Caleb at least wasn't crying, but he looked the color of death.

"I'm so sorry," I said lamely. "It's... it's an awful situation."

"It's all over, too," Caleb said. "We don't blame you, Frank. But once Estelle talks... we're cooked. I know you meant it for the best."

I opened my mouth; but nothing came out. Of course, he was right. They had to face the music. Once Estelle talked, which was going to happen, , the game was up.... And who knew how much the police already knew. They treated me as if I had played a major role—as somebody who had figured out, not the whole truth, but enough of it to make a difference. I was glad that they showed no anger, only a kind of depressed resignation, an acceptance of fate.

When I came out of my own stupor, I tried to be constructive. I told them they should get themselves a good defense lawyer. He might be able to do something for Judd. If Maggie's death was really a tragic accident, perhaps they could avoid the worst of the worst. I didn't bother adding that they were in trouble themselves for trying to cover the whole thing up. I think both Charlotte and Caleb felt relieved, though. Maybe they had a glimmer of hope. What Judd felt, I have no idea. He kept staring down at the ground and blubbering softly.

32

And that was that. In the end, Judd went to jail. I stayed out of the whole affair, after suggesting some names to them—good criminal lawyers. Judd copped a plea and got a fairly light sentence. In a way I suppose that doesn't matter. Even a month in San Quentin would be torture for me, but maybe Judd was made of different stuff. Charlotte won't desert him, I suppose. In the end, too, Charlotte and Caleb were never prosecuted. That must have been part of the deal.

Caleb's wife, though, filed for divorce. My source was Felicity, the woman in the coffee shop, who seemed to know everybody and everything, and for whom gossip was the very elixir of life. Whether he and Charlotte were still together is something I just don't know. The trip to Australia never happened. He did sell his practice to Ryan Dobbs, and he moved away somewhere, perhaps with Charlotte, perhaps not. I heard a rumor that he went to Las Vegas, a far cry from Australia, and was practicing dentistry there. The money from Dobbs went to reimburse the estate of Morris Sylvester—I found that out from Stanley. Some of it, anyway. The rest fell into the hands of Caleb's wife, along with the house and, as Felicity put it, "everything but the kitchen sink." I'm not sure she had accurate information.

I decided, in the light of all these events, that it was time to switch dentists. Yes, Dobbs was just across the street and was apparently quite competent as a dentist.

But I just couldn't stand him. I took my business to Celia's dentist. I have to walk a few blocks to get there, but I figured, why not? The exercise is good for me.

Oh yes, there were two minor mysteries still to be cleared up. One was solved, the other not. The solved one was the mystery client, Mr. Borromeo. I actually met him in the flesh. Borromeo turned out to be Lionel Q. Staunton, an insurance investigator, who had some sort of role in the malpractice case against Dr. Colegrove. He wanted to talk to me about the case, on the assumption that I was Caleb's lawyer in that matter, which I was not, as I told him right away. Out of curiosity, I asked him why he used an assumed name, and the rest of it, in his work. He said it was for reasons "which I do not care to divulge."

"But can I ask," I said, "out of sheer curiosity, why you use that particular name Borromeo?"

He shrugged his shoulders. "No idea. A guy who had this job before me used it. He passed it on to me. Some Shakespeare thing, I think."

I never followed up on the malpractice case. Whether Caleb won or lost. It must have cost him money, one way or the other. Tell you the truth, I wanted nothing more to do with the tangled affairs of Caleb Colegrove. Enough is enough.

The other mystery never did get solved. I never penetrated to the heart of the secret world of the Xyloquex Corporation. What they made, or did, or sold, or what real or imagined function they served—that stayed hidden, at least from me. I suppose I could have investigated, but I never bothered. I just let sleeping dogs lie. I had so many other things to do—a flurry of new business, which is always welcome, and all the little crises of life on the home front, the joys and sorrows and whatever. I simply never had time or inclination to follow up on this strange organization.

It did cross my mind from time to time. About a month or two after the excitement had died down, I wandered over to the building where Xyloquex had had its office, and I noticed that the company was gone. The office was empty. Workmen were painting over the sign on the door. There seemed to be some kind of construction or remodeling going on inside.

I asked a man who worked in the building—an elderly man who sat at a sort of reception desk and who usually had absolutely nothing to do—what had happened to Xyloquex, did he know where they went, and if there was a forwarding address. He put down his magazine, squinted at me, shrugged his shoulders and said, he didn't know nothing about that, they just moved away, and did I have business with them, which I didn't. He said he heard a rumor, that they moved to Cedar Rapids, Iowa, but didn't know for sure. I could have gone to the manager of the building, whoever that was, or the owner, to find out where they went, whether they really were in Cedar Rapids, Iowa, and anything else about them. But I have to admit, I never followed up.

I immersed myself in my work—work with good, honorable clients, clients who paid their fees on time, clients without dead bodies cluttering up their lives... well, that isn't quite correct, because I do so much estates work: there were dead people, to be sure, but they died a natural death. Life is too short, I thought, to spend time searching for Xyloquex. Whatever they are doing, whether it is sending off drones, running a hedge fund or a Ponzi scheme, or some other racket—or even some legitimate business—at any rate, they're doing it somewhere else, maybe in Iowa, but not in San Mateo, California, if they're doing anything at all.

The painting and the construction didn't take very long, and a new tenant moved it. The sign on the door said, Dr. Kenneth Wasserflut, D.D.S., pediatric ortho-dontist. A man who does braces, who helps adolescents with their bite. In my day, people took the bite the good

Lord gave them and had to be satisfied. But times have changed. Apparently, Dr. Wasserflut has a flourishing practice. Felicity, at the coffee shop, says so. One of the dental assistants, who came in regularly for coffee, told Felicity all about it. She also told Felicity that Dr. Wasserflut was young, good-looking, and divorced.

All this from Felicity, as she poured my coffee one morning. I was eating a blueberry scone, in memory of poor Maggie. I personally don't need a pediatric orthodontist. No doubt lots of people do. In any event, I wish him well. I hope he never finds a dead body in his bathroom. The chances are he won't. Lightning never strikes twice. At least not in San Mateo, California.

Also by Lawrence Friedman, more QP Mysteries, in the series *The Frank May Chronicles:*

Death of a Wannabe

An Unnatural Death

The Book Club Murder

Death of a One-Sided Man

About the author

Lawrence Friedman is a professor of law at Stanford University. He teaches courses in American legal history and law and society. He is the author of *A History of American Law*, *Crime and Punishment in American History*, *The Human Rights Culture*, and *Total Justice*, among other works. He has also published *Dead Hands: A Social History of Wills, Trusts, and Inheritances*, a subject which is the backbone of Frank May's (fictional) practice.

Visit us at *www.qpbooks.com.*